ADDRESS BOOK

BIOGRAPHY

NEIL BARTLETT lives in London with his partner James Gardiner. His first novel, the queer love story *Ready To Catch Him Should He Fall*, was written in a council flat on the Isle of Dogs, published in 1990, and translated into five European languages. His second, *Mr. Clive and Mr. Page*, was nominated for the Whitbread Prize in 1996; his third, *Skin Lane*, was shortlisted for the Costa Award in 2007; his fourth, *The Disappearance Boy*, earnt him a nomination as Stonewall Author of the Year in 2014.

You can find out more about Neil and his work, and contact him, at www.neil-bartlett.com

Praise for ADDRESS BOOK

'The rooms where we live out troubled, anxious lives are slovenly or crazy-clean, are as spacious as our desires and as cramped as our frustrations. As a man of the theatre, Neil Bartlett knows how to fill a bed-sit with love or malice, how to elevate a neighbour boy into a military saint, how to find in a dirty mattress a platform for redeeming passion. He is an all-seeing wizard.'
EDMUND WHITE

Neil Bartlett writes beautifully about hope & belonging—and this new book from him is something to really look forward to.
DAWN FRENCH

'Neil Bartlett's astonishing novels have always seemed content to stand on the edge of the party, like the elegant gay uncle content to entertain and startle any who approach. With Address Book he sheds his jacket to get on down. This is a cleverly structured, funny then deeply moving novel about connections, sympathy and the traces left by our lives and loves. This is a novel for anyone who has ever mourned in silence, a book for anyone who has wondered about that well dressed man next door but one.'
PATRICK GALE

'Bartlett is a pioneer on and off the page and we are lucky to have him telling our stories.'
DAMIAN BARR

'Neil Bartlett is a peerless chronicler of queer lives lived— past and present. Address Book is peopled with lovers, battlers, ghosts, penitents, adventurers, and optimists. We're lucky to have this book.'
NIVEN GOVINDEN

NEIL BARTLETT
ADDRESS BOOK

INKANDESCENT
Published by Inkandescent, 2021

Text Copyright © 2021 Neil Bartlett
Cover Design © 2021 Justin David

A CIP record for this book is available from the British Library

ISBN 978-1-912620-12-8 (paperback)
ISBN 978-1-912620-13-5 (ebook)

1 3 5 7 9 10 8 6 4 2

www.inkandescent.co.uk

'This was my bedroom.'

'This? When?'

'When I lived here.'

HAROLD PINTER, *The Room*

14 Yeomans Mews

Tomorrow, everything will be different. There'll be a brand-new care-team for me to head up—a brand new hospital whose corridors I'll need to learn how to navigate—and yet another set of protocols for me to get familiar with I'm sure. But tonight, here I am; seated in the middle of my living-room floor, surrounded by boxes and files, still procrastinating over what to take with me and what to leave behind. It's twenty past eleven, the moving van is booked for seven o'clock tomorrow morning—and here, between my fingers, is a small piece of thin blue paper.

When it first slipped out from between the pages of my old address book, I had no idea what this piece of paper was. But then, as soon as I unfolded it, I remembered everything. His handwriting; his address, and all eleven digits of his phone-number.

Arriving at the train-station, that Saturday morning.

§

Everything is quiet, and I'm fifteen.

When I get to the ticket-hall, the tiles of the floor are still all wet and shining. I'm clearly going to be the first person to walk across them this morning, and so I stop for a moment to gather my nerve. While I stand there in the doorway, I can hear myself starting to mutter something under my breath; *Andrew,* I seem to be saying. *My name is Andrew.*

I sound like I'm trying to convince myself of something.

Or maybe I sound like an anaesthetist does, in the ICU, when they lean forward and ask you to please start counting backwards from twenty.

When they want you to let go.

Now, my feet are stepping forward; they are starting to make their way across a skin of evaporating water. And now, I can see my hands resting side by side on the shelf in front of the ticket-office window. What am I trying to say to the man behind the glass? Ah yes, of course; the name of my destination. The word I've been practising in my bedroom every night for the last two weeks. Twickenham, I say. Or at least, I try to say it—I try to heave the word up out of my throat at least twice, but for some reason it doesn't want to move—and so I cough, and try again. I'd like a cheap day return, I say; A cheap day return, please, to—but at this point my throat closes up completely. The man behind the window leans forward, and he asks me to slow things down a bit. I do what I'm told—and that seems to work, because the next thing I can see is my fingers sliding a sequence of coins through the gap at the bottom of the glass, and the man's fingers pushing my two cardboard train-tickets back towards me in return. I blush, say thank you—and then keep those two precious rectangles of cardboard squeezed tightly in my hand as I head back across the tiles and then turn left towards the ticket-barrier.

The water's mostly gone by now, I notice. I keep my head down, and avoid making eye-contact with the man at the barrier.

Now, I'm out in some sunlight—and finally starting to breathe properly. I find a bench, lean myself back against a patch of already-warm brick wall, and discover that my shirt—my best shirt—is already starting to stick to my back. I look away to my right. Down the tracks, I begin to see a dot, shaking in the heat.

I want this dot to hurry up.

I want it to burst into being a train, and save me.

I know what day of the week this is, because my schoolboy trips up to London were always on a Saturday, even during the holidays. And if I was still fifteen, then the heat that's making my shirt stick to my back already must be happening on the morning of the first or second Saturday of August, 1974. All of that, from one small piece of pale-blue paper.

§

I'd actually met John two weeks earlier, in the gents toilets that used to be down a sharply turning flight of stairs just opposite platform nine at Waterloo Station. We'd both been washing our hands, and the first thing that I can remember catching my eye about him was his long and sun-tanned fingers. They were so very brown, you see, and they looked so strong. Also, there was his ring. It was a gold ring, on his left-hand little finger, with a small black stone in it. As I stared, that sharp black eye had started staring right back at me, as if it somehow already knew what my fifteen-year-old self was after.

The hands stopped moving—and before I could look away, it was John himself who was making eye-contact. He used the mirror to do it, the one they had running in a strip along the top of the washbasins—and he somehow managed to arrange all of the angles so that our eyes met exactly. And it wasn't a question, the way John looked at me; it was a statement.

I felt a kick, somewhere down between my legs—and then I can remember John keeping his eyes locked onto mine, and smiling at me as he shook the water off his hands. And that shocked me, because smiling wasn't what I was used to on these occasions; I felt my face starting to redden—I was a terrible blusher, at fifteen—and then I just sort of stood there, I think, with my own hands dripping uselessly into the washbasin. The muscles in my throat, of course, were starting to knot themselves right up again.

A persistent and involuntary cricopharyngeal spasm, I would label that contraction of my throat-muscles now.

John turned his back. And then, he dried his hands—and left, closing the door to the gents behind him.

As it happened, there was no one else around; no one, to make me feel that I had to hurry with my next move. I dried my hands for a bit—the towel was useless, I remember, all hot and stiff and unhelpful when you pulled it down to try and find a clean bit—and then—well, then I expect I went back to the basins and soaped and washed my hands all over again. That was my usual routine; I would have been hoping, you see, that the door John had closed behind him was somehow going to swing back open all by itself, and that this older man with his suit and gold ring would just walk back in and make everything happen. Make everything happen, without my ever having to be responsible for what any of it looked or felt like.

However, on this occasion, the older man didn't. The door stayed shut, no matter how many times I glanced up in the mirror or pulled down at the towel.

And so—eventually—I must have given up, because the next thing I can remember is my fifteen-year-old self standing out on the station concourse, just by the top of those stairs. There were eyes and hands absolutely everywhere, up there—all moving about in different directions—and I suppose I must have been staring at as many of their owners as I could, while at the same time trying to make sure that my searching didn't look too obvious. However, no matter how hard I stared, I still couldn't make a single one of these hurrying faces or pairs of hands belong to the person I was looking for.

And then I found him. He was the only still figure in that entire, heaving place—and he was standing directly under the famous Waterloo clock, with his back fully turned again, and his hands clasped neatly behind him.

Those beautiful, sun-tanned hands.

19

That heavy, slow-moving clock.

And now, of course, I wonder what John can have possibly been thinking. I wonder what on earth can have been going through his twenty-nine-year-old mind as he placed himself right in the middle of all that chaos and waited to find out if I'd followed him. I mean, he must have known how old I was, because there's no mistaking fifteen-year-old skin, is there? And, like I say, this was happening in 1974, so if any single one of those hurrying people had realised what was going on between the two of us, then their reactions would more than likely have been as ugly as they would have been swift. If—that is—they had been able to read what was written in blood across my teenaged face, as I stood there and stared at John's back, and his hands, and breathlessly willed him to turn around and find me.

Was he thinking of walking away, I wonder? Of giving up, and just getting back to work?

Was he hard, too?

I stood there for quite a long time, I think. And then—then, John did turn around. And despite the crowds, he somehow repeated that extraordinary trick he had of being able to hook his eyes directly into yours. He smiled, even more broadly than before, and the next thing I can remember happening is that I made my way towards him in an absolutely straight line. Which is impossible, given how crowded the station was that lunchtime—but honestly, that's how I remember it happening. I can even see myself doing it; I can see myself, walking towards John across the concourse, and as I watch my face being reeled in by his it's somehow as if everybody in the crowd has been magically instructed to get out of my way. It feels as if it is John himself—John, and his steady smile—who are making this extraordinary thing happen.

It feels as if everybody else there, suddenly isn't quite there at all.

It feels as if he's made me invisible.

I'm going to stop for a minute now. I'm going to put this piece of paper safely back between the pages of my address book, and then I'm going to pour myself a glass of wine.

If I can remember which of these boxes I've packed my wineglasses in, that is.

§

Damn. My phone says it's ten past midnight already.

§

We're standing about two feet apart now, and we're face to face. All of the Waterloo people are still busy walking and talking everywhere around us, but still, none of them seem to be taking any notice. I think I can remember trying to smile myself, at this point, like an actual adult. Or at least like my idea of one. John and I swap names—and I suddenly realise that I've never done

21

this before. None of the other men I've met has ever made me admit that the boy doing the staring and the boy with my name are the same person. My throat snaps shut; no wonder then that it's now John who does all the rest of the talking. He's working just across the road from the station, he tells me, in a church just over the way—and he uses the church's name as if I ought to have heard of it. I haven't, of course, but I nod anyway. And then John says it's a shame, because he only has a quick break for lunch, today, and so he can't stop or do anything just now. And I nod again, because I know what he means when he says that, because I've done plenty of things with men in public toilets before—but at the same time, I don't really know what he means at all; I mean, I don't know where this is going, or what he wants me to say— and so next, there's quite a long pause in our conversation. And then—right out there under that ridiculous great hanging clock that they still have at Waterloo, the one that still always looks to me as if it's about to come crashing down and start killing people—yes, right out there in the middle of the main concourse at Waterloo Station, right in the midst of all of those hurrying people, this handsome, sun-tanned and considerably older-than-me young man says again that he thinks it's a shame he's working just now, but that another time, he'd like to be able to invite me back to his house.

And that stops everything.

Because I really don't know what *that* sentence means.

Because where I come from, that's not what houses are for.

My throat stays closed. John doesn't say anything either, but then—almost as if he's realised it's now or never, and that I might be about to lose my nerve—he reaches inside his jacket. He produces a little black notebook, and a fountain pen—the book has soft leather covers, I notice, like skin, and the pages all have gilt edges—and then John licks his finger, and finds an empty page, and he starts to ink something across the pale blue paper in four separate lines. The strokes of his pen are hard, and fast, and exact—and now, as I watch him do that again, after all these years, I notice that he's writing down all of his details for me exactly like a Junior Doctor writes out a prescription. I mean, with that specific kind of haste which isn't actually hasty or careless at all.

The kind of haste where every word matters.

John puts his pen away, and tears out the page from his book. He checks that the ink is dry, folds the page in half, and holds it out towards me. He's put his phone number at the bottom, he says, and sure, I can hear myself saying, I'll try and call you tomorrow.

What kind of fifteen-year-old agrees to go home with someone he's never met before?

A fifteen-year-old who's ready.

§

Phone boxes always smelt terrible. They stank of sweat, of piss—of cigarette-smoke—of all the other people who'd ever been in there before you. Also, the doors had this unnerving habit of swinging silently shut, like they wanted to trap you.

I'd laid my bike down in a patch of long grass—I'd cycled to a phone box that was right across town, and so was nearly out in the countryside—and now I was inside, and already breathing hard, and getting myself all ready for the call with a stack of ten-pence pieces. I had my piece of blue paper there with me, naturally, and had already got it unfolded and propped up next to the coins. I'd long since memorised everything that was on it, but I still wanted the strokes of John's handwriting there in plain sight.

For the cycle-ride, I remember, I'd hidden the piece of paper down the side of one of my socks.

I dialled his number—a different hole for each number, you had to use—and then, at the very last minute, just as I was struggling to get my ten pence piece into the slot in time, I remember feeling as if my fingers had suddenly become somebody else's. I remember smelling some previous caller's breath on the receiver, and hearing my own breath coming back down the line at me like surf. I remember thinking: are you supposed to say your name, in case he doesn't remember who you are? And then, quite naturally and calmly, John took over.

Just let me check, he said.

Yes, he said; it looks like the weekend after next should be fine.

Do I really remember his voice unknotting my larynx at that point—or is that just what's happening to me now?

I can certainly remember John's instructions. I suppose that's because of how clearly he delivered them, like it was going to be the simplest thing in the world for me to leave my address after breakfast and then arrive at his by lunchtime. Oh, it's easy—he said—you just get on your usual train for London, but hop off at Clapham Junction. Once you're there—he said—look up on the departure boards for anything that's going west marked Twickenham—and don't worry about the train's final destination—he said—just look out for that one name. Twickenham trains run all the time—he said—and once you're on one all you have to do is sit tight and count to seven. First there's Putney, and then Barnes, then Mortlake; there's Richmond, then North Sheen, then St. Margaret's. And then—hey presto—there's me. Come straight out of the station, turn left, and I'll be parked just across the road. Okay?

I remember a slice of sunshine coming in through a dusty window, and moving very slowly across my lap.

I remember watching my legs cross and uncross themselves, and being amazed that there was no-one else in the compartment to see me doing that.

I remember the train slowing down—and I remember especially how strange it was to see the word I'd been muttering in my head all week finally materialising; how strange it was to see it in big black capital letters, sliding past the window.

I remember the catch of that compartment window, as I struggled to pull it down in time, and also the metal of the doorhandle outside. I remember the metal of that handle being as hot beneath my hand as the rib of a panting dog, or a strange man's cock.

Time for another drink.

§

It *is* easy. Walking across the road to his car seems a much simpler operation than crossing those tiles had been this morning—but then, at the very last minute, I mess things up. I go round to the passenger side of the car, like John has told me to, and that's all fine—but then, when I actually get inside, the black, woven strap on the seat-belt feels suddenly way too hot and flexible. It makes me blush again, and fumble. It makes me think of skin— of the covers of his little black notebook—and now that both the car doors have swung shut, I suddenly feel like I'm back in that telephone box again. I can literally smell it—smell all of that trapped breath, and panic—and also I can see John's hands taking a firm hold of the steering wheel, and there's that ring again. It's winking at me.

I feel I badly need to create a barrier between John's hands and my face—and so I use the only thing I have. I start talking, much too loudly—the extra volume, of course, is because I'm trying to keep my throat open—and eventually I do manage to fill the air between my face and John's hands with a layer of protection. I fill it with words about my school, and the train, and the small town I've just come from. I think I possibly even talk about my parents—and all the time, outside of the slowly-moving car, I can see that the August sunshine is starting to hammer down almost vertically, and that it's drawing a hard white line around the edges of absolutely everything. And because of that, even though I'm talking out loud, I can also hear a voice that's located only in the back of my head, and this second voice is saying to me, *Andrew, you do know this is actually happening?* It says those words several times—and I recognise it, because of course it's the same voice that I'd used on myself in the ticket-hall, when I was worrying about whether to put my feet down on the skin of water stretched over those tiles.

Eventually, I manage to look away from the white light outside the windscreen and back across at John. I look at his hands, first, on the steering wheel, and then, gaining confidence, I move my eyes up to his face.

The kick between my legs comes even harder this time. John is watching the road, obviously, but I can see that he's smiling all the same.

I shift in my seat, to try and hide myself.

My shirt is sticking to the small of my back again.

We turn left. There's a curve in the road, lined with some

houses—and they're big old-fashioned houses, not the small modern ones that we have back at home—and then there is a dual carriage-way, cut off from us by a set of traffic lights. There are some bright, dusty trees, close by the road—and now we're turning left again, because the lights have finally gone green. And then, suddenly, there's a plane—an aeroplane, huge—and so close overhead that it seems to fill the whole of the windscreen. I duck, and John laughs. He tells me that Twickenham is right under the Heathrow flight-path; sometimes, he says, there are great queues of the things, whole rows of them hanging up above his house like some sort of giant waiting birds, but that you get used to the noise eventually. Next, there are some big dusty trees again—behind a high wire fence, this time—and then we go left, and right, and left. There's a row of modern-looking flat-roofed houses—and these ones *are* a bit like ours at home, all small and tidy and predictable—and John tells me this is just around the back of where he lives. Then, before I'm quite ready, the car is parked. And here is that seat-belt again, with the fleshy strap that won't quite behave itself between my fingers.

John gets out first.

I remember this next bit as all being in especially vivid colour, for some reason, like one of my grandfather's home movies. The ones he used to show us on Sundays, after lunch.

First, John and I are ducking under some kind of wooden arch or pergola—and then we're coming out onto a bright green lawn that's dotted with still-young trees. I'm two paces behind him, now. The lawn seems to belong to some sort of a communal garden, filling up the space between the two rows of houses which make up John's address—and look, there's a neighbour, across the way, doing some sort of watering with a hose. Because of all this over-exposed sunlight, the water that he's spraying over his flowers is turning into something else entirely. Diamonds, I think. They're certainly making a rainbow. And while I'm noticing this, the man starts waving and calling out a cheery hello—and not just to John, but also it seems to the person walking two paces behind him. As if everything in this sunshine is normal, and all three of us are in the right place at the right time.

John doesn't miss a step.

In fact, he waves right back—and I suppose I must have been looking down at my feet by this point, because what I'm noticing now is that the path which crosses John's grass is made up of exactly the same sort of concrete slabs that we have dividing our front lawn back at home. For some reason, noticing this makes me hold my breath again. We turn left, and I follow John's feet. There are more flowers now on either side of us—fat pink hydrangeas, and some red and white geraniums—and now I must be looking up and ahead of me again, because I can see that John's front door is painted black all over. There's a brass door-knocker, and the house number is in brass too—whereas at home, people ring the bell, and the numbers are just white plastic.

I decide I'm going to try and stop counting all the differences.

John stands aside; there's a step you have to take, he says—and he's right, because I can see that to get fully inside John's house you have to get your feet up and over an odd little raised threshold, which means I'm going to have to watch myself and not stumble. And now John is saying, you go first, and I'm saying, thank you—and look, my feet are doing what they're told.

§

Because of all that dazzle from the water, and the sunshine, everything in here seems dark.

I can see a dining table, with a few too many chairs around it, and now, as my eyes start to gradually adjust, I can make out some sort of a big wooden chest or cabinet. It's very large, and very locked-looking. To the left, there is a piano. Yes—really; right in the middle of John's living-room, there is a jet-black grand piano, which is not something that I knew before today anybody could actually have in their home. Because of its colour, it seems to be soaking up all the noise in the room. It also seems to be collecting all the available light; the lid, for instance, is a gleaming pool of flat, black oil—and I can see that there's a piece of music, floating in it, which I suppose must be something that somebody has lost or forgotten. Behind the piano, there is something else, almost as big as a person. This mystery object is wrapped in a dark blue blanket, tied with a belt and leaning up against the very far wall.

I don't ask.

I don't ask, because I need to concentrate. I say my name again—in my head—but it doesn't really help. At this point John puts his bunch of keys down, and the noise of metal meeting metal brings me back to myself. I turn around, and watch his feet going first up the stairs.

On the landing, there's a bathroom—John points that out in case I need it, I suppose—and then he tells me that the next doorway along is just his spare room. Through the open doorway, I can see a left-open suitcase, and piles of clothes. These things have all just been left sitting out on the bed, and they're clearly all waiting for something to happen to them, but I don't ask what any of that means either.

And then here, at the end of the landing, is the door to John's bedroom.

The door opens, and everything is white. White walls, white wardrobe doors, white bed—and opposite the bed, there's a big piece of mirror, a mirror which has somehow got me trapped inside of it already. I turn away, because I'm not quite ready for that. There are some thin white curtains in front of the window just by the bed, I notice, and they're moving very, very slowly.

Next, there are fingers, undoing buttons, but I'm not sure now if this is John undoing me, or me undoing him. Then, we are both taking off our trousers—and now I'm turning away again, because John is bending over and taking off absolutely every-thing. His trousers, and his socks, and then his pants—and this is something else that I've never seen before, because suddenly he stops being brown all over. Next, there is a duvet—and we only have sheets and blankets, at home—and John is reaching over and dragging this great white thing onto the floor with just the one hand. He does it in one go, just like he tore that page out, and the sudden strength of his arm as he does that makes my throat contract. Next, I can feel the bed-sheet, and it's very cool and smooth beneath my skin. Those white window-curtains are right next to me, now—easily within reach, should I want to stretch out a hand and touch them—and they have shadows moving through them in long, slow waves. The window itself has been left ajar, and the air that's coming in from the garden and sunshine outside feels odd, as if it was somehow both warm and cool at the same time. Then, John starts to touch me; on my feet, first of all, because now I'm lying on my back, and John is standing at the foot of the bed. I know that I'm naked, just like he is, and that he's looking me up and down while he strokes my foot—and I really want to look back up at him while he does that, but I can't. Not yet. And so instead of looking up at him I turn my head to the side and watch the shadows move through those curtains. They are moving very gently—even carefully—like his hand—and the air that is touching them is touching me all over too. And now, finally, I do manage to look up into John's face. And again, just like the first time, the very first thing that he does for me is smile. And I realise now—and I mean *now*, here, in the middle of my living-room floor, in the middle of the night—it isn't the fact that I'm doing all of this in a house for the very first time that is making my fifteen-year-old self feel so astonished; what is astonishing, is that somebody is teaching him that it's quite alright to smile.

The first part of our lovemaking I remember as happening in complete silence. But later on—after half an hour, perhaps—I can very definitely hear myself starting to make a lot of noise. I start to make sounds that I don't think I've ever made before, and that bewilders me. The sounds arrive in the room without my even being sure that it's my own throat that's producing them, and I think I flounder a bit at this point, and maybe even call out for help. When this happens, John doesn't stop. He is using his mouth on me now, and better than anybody's ever done it before; somewhere low down inside my body, I am beginning to feel sensations that are much too large to stay put. I can feel them getting impatient. They are demanding to be acknowledged—and as my back starts to arch and hollow in response, I get the idea that these sounds or feelings of mine are like those planes that John has told me are always lining up over the roof of his house. Except these planes of mine aren't high; they're deep. In fact, they're as deep as you can go without coming out the other side. I start to pant, and next—well I really don't know how else to describe this to you, even though I'm someone who has worked in hospitals all his life, and so ought to be thoroughly familiar with the details of what happens to a body when it starts to feel like somebody else's—next, my younger self arches his back even further, and opens his throat, and begins to sing.

John still doesn't stop what he's doing—but with his spare hand, he does reach up and brush his fingers across my opening mouth. Two of them slip inside me, and he hooks them against my teeth.

When he does this, I understand. John is reminding me that the bedroom window next to us is still ajar, and that the water across the way may still be turning into diamonds above those brilliantly-coloured flowers. But he isn't telling me to stop; he is telling me to keep going. Just quietly. He is telling me that I can signal to those waiting planes any time I want; in fact, he is encouraging me to bring them in to land. He is telling me that nothing needs to stop me now, least of all myself. He is telling me that this sunshine, and my throat, and my voice, are all mine. Andrew, he says, not looking up from his work. *Andrew.*

I come.

§

We all have to leave our childhood selves behind. To abandon ourselves, in a way—and I sometimes wonder if that's why we're all so obsessed with TV shows and stories that take us back into somebody's past and then at some crucial point snap right around to reveal the terrible wound or abuse that is then supposed to explain everything that ever happened to that person afterwards.

Well, just to be clear: this picture of my fifteen-year-old self involuntarily arching his back in John's sun-filled August bedroom is not a picture of abuse at all. I mean, listen to those sounds that I'm making—to those long, straying notes, played *pianissimo*, fingered right up high on the neck of a double bass.

They're wonderful. Wonderful.

How strange it is to be remembering those sounds tonight. In the middle of a pandemic, when once again what you have to fear most from a stranger is his touch, or breath.

Tonight, when I'm about to make another journey into the unknown.

§

Afterwards, John found me looking at that piece of music, the one which had been left out on the lid of his Steinway. The notes were all just flocks of birds on wires, to me, something written in a foreign language entirely, and I suppose he must have seen that from the way I was staring at them. And he could so easily have left it at that, I think, so easily have just asked if I wanted a coffee or something—but instead, John came up quietly behind me, and—stroking the back of my neck while he did it, softly tracing the line of the bones with one expert finger—he told me in that marvellous quiet voice of his what it was that he did for a living. He played in an orchestra, he told me, the double bass—and here he gestured across the room and introduced the big vertical package leaning up against the far wall to me quite formally, as if the instrument wrapped inside the blue blanket was actually another person, and one whose company he loved. And then he told me that the music I was looking at was the score of the piece he was currently rehearsing. That's what he'd been doing in Waterloo, he said—rehearsing with his orchestra, in St John's church, across the road. The flocks of perched birds were all the different parts, he told me—moving his finger from my neck to the page, now—and the notes taking flight from that five-rowed set of wires down there at the bottom were his. Next time, he said, he'd unlock his big old-fashioned gramophone for me, play me a recording of the piece so that I could hear how all the different parts fitted together. Then he shook his keys, and said it really was time for me to start my journey home.

I wanted to ask him what it felt like, to be able to read music; to ask him what it felt like, to know that when you sat down in a room the sounds of all those birds were actually there in the air already, just waiting for you to invite them into your fingers. I wanted to ask him if life was like that. I wanted to know if everything that was ever going to happen to me was actually all there in the air already, but that I just had to learn how to read it, or maybe just be in the right room at the right time.

I look down at my shaking hand, and at this empty wine-glass, and it occurs to me that if I wanted to dial John's number, I wouldn't even have to consult my piece of paper. No; I could get up off the floor, find my phone, and my fingers wouldn't even hesitate.

People think it's your mind that remembers, you see. But actually, it's your body.

§

John and I carried on seeing each other for almost three decades. He got to watch me grow up, which delighted him, and—in return—his was the first body I ever got to see change and grow older. I don't know how many times exactly he picked me up from that parking bay opposite Twickenham station and took me back to his little house on Yeoman's Mews while I was still at school— at least four or five times, I reckon. Later, when I was doing my medical degree and first internships, I used to go and hear him play with his orchestra. He even took me to a rehearsal at St John's, once—but after whatever rehearsal or concert it had been, when we were driving back home through the night with the double-bass strapped in beside him and me parked in the back seat— I stroked *his* neck, then—we always used to talk the miles away. Or rather, I talked, and John listened, because listening was another of his gifts. I'd tell him all about my training—about my ideas—and about all the places I was going dancing in, I expect, because I was quite the clubber in my twenties. About all the differences I was going to make to the world. And perhaps I only feel like this because of the move—but honestly, that confident, late-night, medical-student version of myself now seems even further away than does the stammering schoolboy. He seems so sure of where he's heading.

John died of AIDS; of the plague. It must have been when I was still in my mid-forties, I reckon, around 2005, after that particular virus had been with us for merely the first twenty of its disgusting and hateful years. He and I had almost lost touch, by then; John had moved up to Scotland, to work with a new orchestra, and I was still here in London—at St Thomas's, first of all, and then at U.C.H.—and the two of us had really got down to Christmas cards as our main means of contact. Indeed, I only heard that John was dead when a mutual friend of ours sent me a copy of his obituary from a music magazine. The picture that accompanied the article was lovely; John was still smiling, of course, straight into the camera—and still wearing his ring. You could see that he was still tanned from whatever tour the orchestra had just been on. He always did somehow find the time to keep his skin dark and his arse bone-white, no matter how many concerts he had to rehearse for.

About a year later, I tracked down and ordered a CD that featured John playing Bach in a church in Edinburgh. I opened the Amazon envelope, scanned the notes on the back of the CD until I found John's name—traced it, with the tip of my finger—but I'm afraid I wasn't then brave enough to go through with tearing off the cellophane and actually putting the disc into my machine. I suppose I thought that hearing those beautiful sounds coming from the same hands and fingers that had once played me would have been just too brutal an experience. However, it must still be around somewhere, that CD—I'm sure I must have packed it with the others. Perhaps at my new address I'll finally get to tear open that cellophane, and hear him again.

I think maybe we all have places that we need to revisit in our lives—places that we need to go back to, in order to remind ourselves how the hell we got from there to here.

Putney, then Barnes, then Mortlake; Richmond; North Sheen; St Margaret's.

Twickenham.

Right; I'm going to fill two more boxes with files, and then the rest will have to wait till it's light. The van's not due until seven after all.

103 Cavendish Mansions

Well you never expected to end up in a place like this. Never mind a room of one's fucking own et cetera, they've given you a hallway, kitchen, bathroom, front-room *and* a back bedroom. And in EC1 would you fucking mind—I mean, right on the Clerkenwell Fucking Road. You'll even be able to walk home from Heaven. Oh yes; no more hunting for the night-bus fare home for you, my girlie; no more asking can anyone lend us a couple of quid please for when Ms Belinda Carlisle or whoever it is doing the last track of the night finally calls time on her vocals and the lights come crashing back on for everybody's bedtime. When Our Miss Roberta rattles her ice and says Jeffrey my darling the last round of the night is yours I believe, you'll be able to answer certainly my darling, vodka tonic I believe Madam is drinking?

Miss Roberta. The Mother of us all.

Shame the six-footer you were dancing with that night hasn't turned up yet, by the way. The trainee doctor, with the eyes. What was his name? Anthony? Adam? Andrew. Maybe he didn't hear your address properly—the music does get loud in that bar at the back. You should have written your details on the top of your fag-packet like Miss Roberta always does. Still, you never know;

maybe he'll turn up one night next week, knock you up in the early hours and surprise you. He looked like he might be quite surprising, actually, underneath that shirt. And aren't all doctors good with their hands?

Anyway; plenty more trade in the sea, as Miss Roberta always says. Speaking of whom, note to self: remember to ask Mother if that really was Mr Jarman in the back bar on Friday, and is it true that he's looking for people for a new film. It'll be all the usual, I suppose. Boys in sheets, boys in slow-motion et cetera. Bet he'd love the new tattoo on my shoulder though. Jean Cocteau Is God.

§

Fuck me but it's hot again tonight. Even lying here with nothing on. I suppose I could try getting this nasty old bedroom window unjammed again, to get some air in, but then the noise from the traffic on Rosebery Avenue would be even worse. Three ambulances already I make it tonight—three of the bastards, right outside my window. Making the bedroom ceiling go all light-show, flashes of electric blue then back to street-lamp yellow. There's an idea for the dance-floor.

Of course I've never actually had to do that bit, thank Christ. Not yet, anyway. Holding somebody's hand in the back of an ambulance, honestly, I do think—

I think it must be the worst thing fucking ever.

Looking down at somebody's face, and realising that he

doesn't even know you're there. Going through red lights at four in the morning, swerving round corners till you're sick. Left, right, left—plus all the time knowing what the ward at the Middlesex is going to look like when you finally get there. All that panic, and the curtains being pulled round, and some fucking orderly in a hurry saying excuse me but are you next of kin? Well, I hope I never have to do it. Visiting people once they're already on the ward is quite bad enough, thank you very much.

Second note to self: find the nearest phone box to this place and call Ivan tomorrow, ask if there's any news of Stuart M. or Keith. And you'd better ask about that Lauren as well, even though you hardly know him. Bound to be bad news by this stage I expect.

God it's funny to be lying face-up on a mattress at this time on a Friday night instead of being in the middle of the dancefloor with everybody. Still, you did promise Miss Roberta you'd make an effort with this week's DHSS and cut down. The boys will still all be there next week. Probably not Trainee Doctor Andrew, though. He said he doesn't go out that often, because of the hours they make them work. For all the exams and whatever, I suppose. Damn.

§

No wonder you don't quite feel that you've moved in yet. Bare walls; bare windows; bare mattress on the floor. Jammed-up

45

old-fashioned window-frames, printing black crosses on your bedroom ceiling. Brand-new Camden Council rent-book, lying right there in the half-dark, next to your Marlboro Lights. That weird dusty smell coming up off the floors still.

This mattress is the only clean thing in here.

Brand-new. Shop-smelling.

Christ, girl; seventy-eight quid—what on earth were you thinking? A hundred quid full stop your Hardship Grant was for moving in here—so who now only has twenty quid and some loose change left in her handbag till next Thursday morning?

§

It was that shop-woman's fault. No really. You were only on the Tottenham Court Road in the first place because you'd been to the clinic in Mortimer Market for a check-up—and since when did a girl like you have the money to go shopping for stuff in places as big and smart as the ones on Tottenham Court Road? But the windows looked lovely, and you thought you might as well have a look around—I mean, you'd never actually bought a bed of your own before, so you thought it would be good to pop in, get a few ideas, then go looking for the actual and affordable thing later. Bethnal Green, Miss Roberta says is always good for second-hand stuff, and it looks like a couple of the buses from round here might go up that way directly. Right from out under your front-room window, for instance; it says the number fifty-five goes up the Clerkenwell Road to Old Street and then all the way over to Dalston and Hackney Downs and whatever. Walthamstow. Maybe you should check that out first thing tomorrow morning. If you're up in time.

Just the one of you is it, sir, the shop-woman said—and in *that* voice, you know? The one with loathing sprinkled on top of every single syllable. Plus the eyes were already up and down you like a rake. Just the one of you, is it, sir, she said, leaning on that last word like she really wanted to spit. And I mean, I was on my own, right? It's not like I was with Miss Roberta or anything, and we were letting our hair down. Or like I was wearing anything particularly noisy that morning, because just your basic 501's and a checked shirt, it was. And my face was pretty much clean. Well alright, maybe a touch of eyeliner from the night before, but still, that shop-woman's mouth was puckering the minute she saw me. Like she really wanted to see some saliva on my face, you know? Like she'd been trained to spot one.

Well let's face it they probably are.

We only have quite a modest selection of single mattresses in stock at the moment I'm afraid, she said, pecking at me already with that fucking metal voice of hers—and that was it. That was the word that really flicked your switch. We only have quite a modest selection of *single* mattresses in stock. Like she was assuming straight away that nobody who looks like me ever went shopping for a double, right? Like she was assuming straight away that nobody who looks like me would ever want to wake up lying next to somebody else. And straight away, there was that voice inside your head again, the rant that seems to be always on the tip of your fucking tongue these days, straight away saying oh sorry, lady, but before you carry on talking to me in that tone of voice, would you maybe like to hear some of our side of the story for a change? Would you maybe like to hear what life is like on the animal's side of the chain-link fencing just for once? Would you like to know about some of the funerals, for instance—or how about the ward-visits? Or I tell you what, perhaps I could tell you all about how many times Miss Roberta's been slammed up against a wall already this year, slammed up against a wall by a total stranger and had her eyes punched out just for how she walks down the fucking street? And now that I've got your attention, perhaps you'd do me the courtesy of looking me in the eye while you wish me off the face of the earth, you cow. You complete, fucking, absolute *cow*.

Sorry. Well at least I only said it to her in my head. And she asked for it.

Shit, I need a fag now.

§

Actually, maybe the way that Tottenham Court Road shop-woman looked at you is the key to this whole fucking nightmare. I mean; maybe that's what people really can't stand. Not so much the disease itself, just the thought of two of us being on the same mattress at the same time. People give so many reasons for the hate, don't they, so many excuses, but maybe what they really can't stand is simply the thought of two bodies lying side by side. I mean, maybe they don't really give a toss what we actually get up to while we're there. Maybe it's really just the thought of us being skin to skin all night that makes them go so cross-eyed and mental and step away from the kiddies you disease-carrying freak.

Sometimes I wish they'd just say it to your face. Just spray it all out, like the shit it is. Just be honest for fucking once, you know?

§

Another siren. Yellow; blue; yellow... And Christ, I'm sweating in here. Don't want to stain anything, do I.

§

So you interrupted her. You interrupted her, and you said out loud, excuse me, but I *was* hoping to look at some doubles. I've just got this flat, you see—you said. From the Council. I've been sleeping around all over the place for the last three and half years—sofas, squats, you name it darling, I've lain on top of it—but last week—you said—they told me I'd finally got to the top of the list. Now, it is on the Clerkenwell Road, this new place of mine, and so yes, it is a bit run down. In fact, Victorian, this block is, according to that very nice lady in the housing office, so who

49

wouldn't be—but the thing is—you said—the bedroom may be small, but it's perfectly big enough for a double mattress. And buggers can't be choosers, can they?

Well, you may as well give as good as you get, as Miss Roberta always says.

She flushed, of course, and looked daggers, but what could she do? The customer is always right, et cetera. So she turned on her heel—and actually, the whole thing was very Rosa Klebb, you know, in the Bond film, that bit where she has those daggers in her shoes—and anyway, off she sets, and straight away she's already started on her spiel. Walking and talking at the same time, she is, walking me right out into the middle of her precious bedroom furnishings department as fast as those crabby little pins of hers can carry her. And gabbling, or what? Christ, I mean proper thirteen to the dozen it was, like she wanted to get it all over with as soon as possible and then give herself a really good wash. Just in case the leaflets are wrong, and you really can catch it just by being in the same room at the same time.

So, anyway, there she was, running all through her list of different models of mattresses and prices like the details were worms and her mouth was a beak—a metal one—and there you were, trailing along behind her, wondering what on earth you were going to do or say once this spiel of hers had run dry. Because you could hear the prices she was listing, and quite frankly they were ridiculous. I mean, they were ridiculous for somebody out shopping on a Camden Council Hardship Grant—and so you decided to turn her voice down in your head.

I mean really just for the sake of keeping your fucking sanity. Except that was when the weird stuff started.

So first, right, the rows of mattresses all started to look the same. Like they were all naked. Or something. Like they were all queuing for the showers, actually, in one of those Belsen films. Anyway; then, they started to look like a colour-chart—you know, one of those things with all the different paints on—except that these were all just different colours of skin. So like they were all Ivory, or Nude, or Tan. Flesh. Or whatever. And of course, the woman's voice was yapping on at you all of the bloody time still, laying down yet more prices and brand-names—and so to try and really blank the sound out completely, you started filling in all of the different little empty rectangles with imaginary bodies. A chest here, a nice pair of legs there—that doctor-boy's shoulders, for instance, but definitely with his shirt *off*, this time—but that got scary, and the rows of beds started to turn into a sort of exploded version of the ward at the Middlesex. Which was bad. I mean, very. And also, the woman's voice kept on getting through the curtains somehow, and the bodies were all sort of slipping onto the floor. And then—and this was even worse, in a funny sort of way—you started to notice all the furnishings. I mean you started to notice that even though the mattresses themselves were all naked and undressed, for instance, the bedsteads underneath them were all standing on some little bit of carpet or whatever, and every bit of carpet also had its very own individual bedside cabinet. You know? So like they'd set it up so that every separate bed was supposed to be in a different actual room or something. Like every bed in the showroom was supposed to be part of somebody's actual life. And some of the cabinets even had little ornaments on them, little pictures or china figurines or whatever, and one of them even had an actual alarm-clock, for Christ's sake, and set to the actual real time. But no ashtrays, you noticed, and no packs of Marlboro Lights; no condoms, and no KY. So like this was all real life, but just not ours. And you were thinking all of that to yourself, when you noticed the photograph.

Which was the last fucking straw, really.

It was a woman, in a swimsuit. In a red swimsuit, in fact, on some sort of a fancy beach, and with the sun coming in through her hair—so sort of like a shampoo advert or something, only she'd been cut out and put in this posh little silver frame. And the point is, she was smiling; smiling like she thought she was your future, only you just didn't know it yet. And while you were thinking about that—about her smile, and what it was trying to tell you—you became aware of this fly, buzzing right in your ear. And this was because the shop-woman had realised that she'd lost you, you see, while you were standing there and staring, and so she'd trotted back to find you—which meant that then, while you were standing there and staring at this photograph of a woman in a red swimsuit who wanted to tell you all about the lovely, happy and predictable life that you and she were going to have together, in the future, you also gradually began to be able to hear Mrs Shop-Woman again, buzzing right in your ear there and getting louder all the time, and it seemed like she was saying, seventy eight pounds that particular model is, sir. Which didn't make any sense at all, at first, because you thought she meant the woman on the beach. But then, it did, because the shop-woman was thinking you were staring at the mattress, you see, not at the photograph at all. And bloody hell you could hear the triumph in her voice. You could hear it; hear that claggy scarlet lipstick beginning to fill in all the little vertical cracks as she smiled— because Mrs. Shop-Woman was sure she'd got you now, you see; she was sure that what with her telling you the exact price of this particular model she was about to make you give up the struggle and admit that her bedroom furnishings department wasn't the right place for someone like you at all, oh no, not in a million years my darling, because obviously you didn't have the right to be there in the first place, never mind the money. Because obviously—*obviously*—you were never going to have a lovely smile like that greeting *you* from a framed photograph on your bedside cabinet first thing in the morning. Oh no. Not in a million years my darling. And so, just to shut her up—just to clean the smile off that pecking, metal, blood-clagged beak of hers—you turned right round and you looked her straight in the face for once and you said in your best posh voice, but I'll take it. You reached right round into your jeans back-pocket, you pulled out your envelope with its five crisp Hardship Grant twenty-pound notes still all lying there inside it, and you fanned them out into Mrs. Shop-Woman's face before she'd even had the chance to get her jaw up off the floor.

No wonder Miss Roberta laughs. No wonder she says Jeffrey my darling, I don't know why you bother doing drugs and alcohol at all. The things you've got going on inside your head, she says, really you should be available on the NHS.

§

Four o'clock in the morning. Or maybe even half past already.

Giving an unfamiliar new address at some big posh sales desk on the Tottenham Court Road—telling the assistant there that certainly you'll able to accept delivery at the specified time; is that what it means, finally having a place of your own?

Or; reaching across the floor in the half-dark, and checking that it's still your name printed in that little window on the dark green Camden Council rent-book—picking it up, and physically checking that the print hasn't rearranged itself into somebody else's name during the sound of that last fucking ambulance; is that what it means? Is that what it feels like, knowing that you finally have a front door of your very own that you can use to shut out all this *shit*? Or, when the two men from the delivery-van take one look at you, and they see your check shirt and your number one crop and your eyeliner, and their faces slam shut—is that what it means, maybe? When their faces slam shut, because oh yes, they know what you are. They've read about you in the papers. When the older one says with that stupid straight-boy smirk of his, sorry mate, we're not allowed to do stairs—knowing full well that there's nothing you can fucking do about it. Or next, when you're wrestling a double mattress up twelve filthy flights of Victorian fucking council-block stairs all on your own, when you're heaving it all the way up to the fucking sixth floor would you mind, with the dead weight of it making you sweat and stumble, with the dead weight of it making the polythene slide under your sweaty hands and making you swear *fuck*—and then, finding the keys (note to self; get those security locks fitted tomorrow)—finally—and then manhandling the fucker in through your very own front door, sliding it across your hall and shoving and pushing it into your very own filthy and empty back bedroom—finally—and tearing the polythene off straight away with your bare hands, and then staring down at it, at this great big flesh-coloured *thing*, staring at it lying there all brand-new and naked-looking in the middle of your otherwise empty and filthy yet also very-own bedroom floor—the only fucking clean thing in here—and also at that moment hearing your breath still heaving from the effort of getting it up the stairs like you had actually just come or something. Or next, when the sight of it lying there starts to make you think about the future—and oh yes my darling, here it comes; here it actually fucking comes, the *point*; when the sight of this empty double mattress lying there on your actual, real and very own back-bedroom floor starts to make you feel that the idea of the Future might be a real actual fucking thing for once in your dancing-queen life; and I mean, like not just some jerk-off or cinema fantasy for once, but real; when, for instance, the sight of the mattress starts to make you think about having two pillows lying side by side in this bedroom—two pillows, in two brand-new pillowcases maybe, lying side by side just like on everybody else's bed—just like in everybody else's real, actual and red-swim-suited lives; two pillows, side by side, with two actual, alive and breathing faces to go with them—side by actual side—well: is that it?

When you're staring at a brand-new double mattress, and the sight of it is making you think about waking up next to somebody else not just one morning, but the next morning after that.

And then, when you find yourself being terrified of that pos-sibility—when you find yourself being terrified of that possibility quite exactly, because you are so sure that the person lying next to you on those pillows is going to get sick, you see, so sure that they are going to get the lesions on their face, or even across those beautiful wide shoulders he had, so sure of that possibility in your mind that you know you shouldn't even try—

Well; is that it?

Is that what having a front door feels like, these days?

§

Christ another siren. Crosses, on your bedroom ceiling.

§

So right, we're agreed; you need to get those security locks on the front door sorted *tomorrow*. Where did that woman in the Housing Office say was the cheapest place to go for that? Somewhere on the Farringdon Road, wasn't it? Oh and by the way, additional note to self: she was kind, that one. Proper old London kind. Telling you you'll be fine up there on the top floor my darling, because it's usually only ground-floor numbers where the Council has trouble with people kicking the doors in and whatnot. But you get yourself a pair of extra mortices anyway my darling, she said, just to be on the safe side—and turning on her proper Comedy Cockney for you she was, proper Dot Cotton voice and everything. Saying don't you tell anybody I said so darling, because officially you can't touch those front doors, not even to change the colour—and then sliding the keys across the counter with a wink.

So you see not everybody in this town works on the Tottenham Court Road. Not everybody these days is like Mrs Shop-Woman-With-A-Beak or those two delivery guys. Not everybody believes what they read in the Mail and Sun and Telegraph Bastards. Some people actually want you to get home safe on the night bus.

Some people are actually still human beings.

And also, if there's any dosh left after you've got those locks, please do get yourself a screwdriver or something, because if you don't get the sash unjammed in here you're going to bloody stifle. Also, some sort of a scraper-thing to get the rest of the paper off the walls in the front room, plus some Polyfilla or whatever to fix the big crack. I reckon there must have originally been a dividing wall between those two windows, and that somebody never fixed the plaster after they'd knocked it out. Probably there must have been another bedroom at the side there, though Christ knows what sort of a shoe-box that would have been for sleeping in. And speaking of fixing things (yes I know this is a list, but there's no way you're going back to sleep with all of this lot running round inside your head) see if the hardware people on the Farringdon Road have any of those little sample tins of paint. Red gloss, ideally. That way, next time you want to tell some piece of possible trade how to find you, some trainee doctor for instance, never mind tearing the top off your fag packet and borrowing a pen from behind the bar, you just tell him to head straight up the Grays Inn Road, turn right at the lights, go first left inside the courtyard and then look right up to the top. The council gives us all regulation black front doors, you can tell him, but since I moved in, things have changed. You can't miss me, because I'm the only flamer here.

Final note to self: do yourself a favour, next week, and find somewhere that does cheap pillows and sheets. Because that doctor-boy may not have turned up yet, but let's face it my darling, it's high time this mattress of yours got christened. And also, eventually, why not a duvet—because it won't stay this hot and sweaty for fucking ever you know.

And it won't be nineteen eighty-seven for ever either.

It can't be.

It just fucking can't be.

As Miss Roberta always says.

103 Cavendish Mansions
(again)

I speak not to living ears, but for those who will come after. To root my tale in time and place, let me say at once that this is the year 1891—and that I have never yet resided at an address this singular. The towering walls of the Mansions here on the Clerkenwell Road—'The Buildings', as we residents call them— are still so recent as to be raw; we have water-closets, and dust-chutes, and the light of a window in every single room—and yet, despite all of this shining newness, my short neighbourhood walk to work takes me down into a world as ramshackle and ancient as any in London. Down there, on those steeply plunging side-streets, all is yet dark and squalid—many residents have no real possessions or security to speak of—while up here, in The Buildings, people set themselves up as if they meant to reside here for ever. One sees children, cooking-pans, canaries—even a cabinet pianoforte, being installed just opposite—though God knows how Sr Capra and his sons managed to haul it up all twelve turns of our narrow-stepped stairs! In truth, <u>everything</u> here speaks of Contradiction.

Dwelling One-hundred-and-three of The Buildings has been my abode for nearly five months now—since the eighth of February, in fact—and yet still this lodger's bedroom of mine feels strange. Often, in the early hours, I must remind myself that it is my own dreams and ambitions that have brought me here, not some other's imperative—and that I, who have so often felt myself a Wanderer in life, have here at last felt some sense of arrival. My school-master's coat fits me well, and in the evenings I am left in peace; Sra Galleatti keeps the children reasonably silent, once dinner has been cleared, and this bed is quite big enough for me to sit up and write here on my Drawing-Board. And the light, of course—and the linen—that rediscovered box, in my suitcase—oh, there have been such marvellous accidents here!

I run ahead of myself—and besides, the word <u>accident</u> surely over-states my case. It makes me think of that poor woman who went beneath a brewer's cart out on Portpool Lane, and of what was done to her body by those dreadful wheels. As I lie here, waiting for the day to fully break, I am sure I do not bleed like that.

The bell of St Peter's calls out; it is five o'clock already, and the city will soon be awake. I teach until two, this afternoon, and the boy is due here at three. Preparations must be made for our final session—and first, I must tell my story. Confession is always good for the soul, is it not—and my mind must needs be clear when he knocks, no less than my heart. Very well then; let us begin with the necessary phrase;

<u>Dominus sit in corde tuo...</u>

§

I dreamt first of being an artist. After leaving home, I attempted several trades, and experimented with several dwelling-places; however, none of them suited. While residing at last in Birmingham, and nearing now both Despair and the age of twenty—and oh, how strange and long ago that summer of '87 now seems—I chanced upon a working-men's library. This lay quite close to my then-current address, and here it became my habit to study whenever I could. Many is the time that I have pored late in the evening over the engraved masterpieces of Rafaello, Signorelli and the divine Buonarotti, gazing at them under those too-dim lights until closing-time sent me away to a single bed. This un-looked-for place of inspiration turned out to be in the vicinity of a Catholic seminary, and later, through a series of chance meetings (forgive me; at this late hour, I needs must summarise) I came within the influence of the Church of Rome. After some struggles, with both myself and others, I promised that Church my life. For a short while during that same hot summer I dreamt even of a vocation; however, my faith found obstacles (again, I needs must summarise—but strange it is to condense so desperate a period of my life into so journalistic a phrase) and I was duly requested to leave. Distracted, and perhaps reluctant to depart a neighbourhood that had once been so filled with Hope, I heard one day of nearby employment. It was at a Chemist's, in Edgbaston, and one that offered Photographic Processing amongst its other services; since I was able to tell him quite honestly that I had made some amateur study of the arts of the camera, the Chemist in question took me on at once. During my first weeks there, I found not a little solace; but soon the hours grew long, and the company stifling. The contrast between my current occupation and the dreams I had aspired to but a few short months earlier became a daily Rebuke to both my mind and soul; I grew to hate the stinking chemicals—yea, hate the very street on which the Chemist's stood! The cast metal of the street-sign—oh, even that sign itself seemed to bear the stamp of imprisonment. However, I now give thanks for all the days I spent incarcerated there. Indeed, it seems to me that my time at that address was not an <u>Inferno</u> after all, but a <u>Purgatorio</u> merely. By increasing my acquaintance with that place where Art and Science meet—I mean a Chemist's dark-room—those long Birmingham days surely paved the road that has finally brought me here. To this blessed day, and to this steadily brightening morning.

I lost my post in Edgbaston though a disagreement with a fellow-worker—again, let us keep things brief—and I went subsequently through dark times. I will not tire you by dwelling upon them here; suffice it to say that they involved Journalism, and that of the most Provincial kind. My resources being by this time almost entirely gone, I applied to various English Catholic charities for some relief—after all, they were not to know that I had once sworn never to willingly enter a Roman establishment again—and besides, Hunger is a great refiner of principles. One of the seven letters of refusal that I received in reply to my applications contained a small and neatly-excised advertisement from a London newspaper; this same cutting informed me that the school attached to a St Peter's Catholic Church on the Clerkenwell Road (London) was seeking a Junior Master; moreover, the Master in question was to be one with not only a native command of English, but also an educated acquaintance with Italian and Church-Latin. The stipend offered was economical, but the advertisement mentioned that accommodation was to be provided close by and all found. At my then lodgings, I had almost no practical means of paying the rent; this same rent was due always on a Friday, and I remember most vividly my landlord's calendar insisting on it's being already a Wednesday morning as I sat and studied that advertisement. I sent off my letter of application by return—but with no great hopes of success, since my Catholicism was lapsed, my Latin rusty, and my Italian acquired mostly from a paper-back Dante. That application was, you might say, an almost-final throw of the dice—and I was astonished to receive such a prompt invitation to interview in reply. I sold my other pair of shoes, so as to afford the train, and took with me only the one suitcase.

As you have probably gathered, I feel now at some distance from the creature I was, when I dreamt chiefly of Our Mother the Church as my home. But I do not regret that younger man's ardour—nor indeed do I regret or scorn the very specific forms that his faith then took. Rome gave me images which I still find valid—and let us not forget that it was in so many ways the time served in Her arms that secured me my employment here on Herbal Hill (that is the proper address of St Peter's School, the door being just around the corner from the Clerkenwell Road itself). Father Ferrari, who is our Head Master here, accepted me as a Catholic from my manner alone, and then said that he was sure my Italian would be adequate. <u>What St Peter's most looks for in a Junior Master,</u> he said, <u>is Stubbornness in the face of a Hard Task. That, Father</u>—I replied—<u>I can most certainly supply</u>.

However, I regret to admit that after this moment of frankness—in my somewhat desperate eagerness to obtain the post—I then went on to embroider my professional experience a little. I described myself as a Writer, when I should have said Journalist, and as an Artist, when all I had truly done was to make some sketches, after the Antique, and then also some strictly private camera-studies in a similar mode. Fr Ferrari rubbed his hands briskly together as I mentioned these things, and offered me the Junior Master's job at St Peter's barely fifteen minutes after I had entered his somewhat cramped and fustian offices.

Do you see now why I see intimate in all this story a certain kind of accidental Providence? Trudging past that baleful iron street-sign every day—making other peoples' dreams emerge out of darkness—bathing all of those relentlessly one-inch squares of Kodak's Patent Photographic Paper in solutions of varying bitterness for hours on weary end—it all, as it turns out, served some Other and Higher purpose! The tricks of Application and Judgement that I learnt in Edgbaston will be the very ones I shall apply this afternoon, for instance—indeed, I am sure it is only in consequence of my learning from Frustration there that I shall have the head both to correctly calculate my distances and to keep my hand quite steady on the shutter-release today. I have seen too many botched Studies emerge from the developing baths, to want to perpetrate any of my own. My hand will hardly shake— the sun will shine—and I shall feel no Shame at all. I swear I shall not, for I vowed to Heaven, on my last night in that Seminary chapel in Birmingham, that I would never again place myself in the way of that most Soul-Destroying and Soul-Damning of emotions. Yea, as I lie here in the first ruddy morning light, I renew that vow with every breath and bone in my body. I shall never speak—or think—of Shame and Him together.

§

As a Youth, my occasional experiments with both my own and others' bodies had been clumsy—and, of course, constrained. However, they had occasioned in me no Natural Disgust. Indeed, my inclination—my Instinct, I would rather say—was to persist in these explorations, and thus to seek out some Person or Persons who might fully reveal to me those joys which my life had, as yet, only hinted at.

It was a strange thing, therefore, when I passed into Young-Manhood, and entered the Birmingham seminary, to hear those same experiments of mine repeatedly named as the surest of all passages to everlasting Condemnation and Hell-Fire.

My last experience of congress—I will not stoop to naming the man, but merely record that the Act took place on a coldly-tiled vestry floor, and that the garments being there unbuttoned were long, and black—that last experience had left me swearing to never again place myself in the way of such clumsiness. It was not so much the pain, as the haste—and especially, the swift turning-away of the man's face, afterwards—that confirmed me in my belief that the act of love—I would rather say, its Rite!— should be held sacred by all who search for Truth in human affairs, and therefore never knowingly cheapened. Later, I began to read on the subject. This was not easy, of course, as an endeavour, using only such public shelves as I had access to; however, I did find some foreign writings to light my way, including those of the New World's Mr Whitman, and also some productions of our own native Mssrs Symonds and Pater. There were also, of course, the Lives of some especially-beloved Artists in which to find Succour, as well as Information. These studies of mine fortified me; I learned that I was not alone on my journey—and indeed, I came to take particular solace in Mr Whitman's notion of the Ideal Friend, a creature who is frequently to be found, by his account, in the very hearts of great cities. This notion of Whitman's was, I must say, not the least of those that spurred me to London when that letter inviting me to interview was slipped beneath my landlord's door.

Since leaving Birmingham, I have kept strictly to my vow. I have had no truck with the Shameful, and have thought it no sin to be Proud of myself, at least in that respect. I have eschewed Scraps, and waited for my invitation to the Feast of Love itself. In fact, right through until this very <u>Anno Domini</u>, I have allowed myself intimacy of almost no kind. There have been thorns a-plenty, to prick me on my road, and on the way to this morning's Gethsemane I have heard laughter and obscenities from several darkened doorways—but I have not broken my vow. <u>Young man, we must all seek to raise ourselves to our highest potential!</u> Fr Ferrari exclaimed to me when he was iterating the principles of his school to me during that first interview—and with that passionate statement of intent I still feel in whole-hearted accord. How can one in any way aspire to teach, if one does not also aspire to Love?

§

My own contribution to the realisation of Fr Ferrari's ideal was to be the teaching of English—specifically, the instruction of the youngest and most recently immigrant of the school's male children in both English Grammar and Basic Pronunciation. To do this, as that advertisement had specified, I needed to know something of the immigrant boys' own tongue in addition to my own. Well, my Italian—like my Religion—may well have been sufficient for an interview, but my first week of teaching soon showed me its limitations! The immigrant families of the Hill (<u>il Quartiere</u>, the boys all call it), traditionally cluster together according to the laws of family origin—and each street is therefore associated with a distinct Italian dialect. There is Calabrian for the ice-cream makers on Saffron Hill, Emilian for the many piano-makers of Little Bath Street, <u>Friulano</u> for the mosaic-cutters further north—and so on. To begin with, I floundered in this Babel; however, it soon became apparent that my pupils accorded my occasionally-mangled attempts at communication the same sort of grudging respect that they accorded my schoolmaster's coat, and I began to feel less anxious. There was even laughter, on some mornings. I had saved my precious (if paper-backed) Dante from the shipwreck of Birmingham, and I now took to reciting from this volume as I walked to work. This helped a great deal; I discovered that the four short corners of my journey—the corners of Laystall, Vine and Bath Streets, and then Back Hill itself—could be traversed in the space of exactly eight reasonably-paced Dantean <u>stanze</u>—and that my pupils and I understood each other considerably better once my mouth and lips had undergone this limbering-up, first thing.

The Hill is a strange neighbourhood to seek to become a part of. I would often on those early walks to work of mine be arrested by features that seemed to have strayed straight from some Roman or Venetian masterpiece—by the face of a <u>Doge</u>, or Prince—only to then see the owner of those same features running for the Dalston-and-Hackney omnibus. I remember sometimes asking myself what world this was, that I now so suddenly found myself attempting to inhabit. I would break off from my muttered Dante—and tell myself that I must not stare.

§

To the main purpose of my tale.

On the morning of our first meeting, all was routine. The bell of St Peter's awoke me as it always does, and then came the sound of the water-closet, followed by that of the faucet in the kitchen—my landlady Signora Galleatti is I am happy to say a great one for cleanliness, and the place always is spot-less. This, despite her having two children, both of whom sleep in the same room as we take our meals in, and a husband who works in a relentlessly filthy trade. My morning cup of coffee that day was presented to me as always, with a faultlessly snowy napkin, and the coffee itself was strong and freshly-boiled. I thanked my landlady in my usual fashion, and she laughed as always to have what she calls her <u>Maestro Inglese</u> address her in her native tongue. However—as always—there was to be no lingering at table; she had her day's labour of starching and ironing to begin (the trade of laundress is almost ubiquitous amongst the wives and mothers of The Buildings) and I had to be down our stairs and turning left onto the Clerkenwell Road at least ten minutes before seven. So far as I remember, I kept my time. I muttered my Dante—we were in the second circle of Hell that morning, with the wind-chased lovers—and as I reached the corner of Herbal Hill the Senior Boy was only just beginning to swing his hand-bell. I skirted the cluster of pupils who were jostling for admission, and exchanged a swift greeting with Miss Deacon (Miss Deacon is my fellow Junior; she teaches drawing and em-broidery, to the older girls). I then hurried up the stairs to com-mence my labours. Perhaps—who knows—I muttered that day's allotted lines from the <u>Inferno</u> again to myself on the stairs, just to make sure my tongue was primed: <u>Amor, ch'al cor gentil, ratto s'apprende...</u>

'Love, that so harshly seizes the unsuspecting heart...'

But I run ahead of myself once more, and must not. Surely I learnt in Birmingham that no image emerges sharply if one's timing is awry.

After the <u>Benedicte</u>, I began our class with my usual greeting—it was returned, as on every other morning, somewhat raggedly—and then, before I began the lesson proper, I followed my greeting with an enquiry as to whether any of my assembled charges might enlighten me as to why the youngest son of the Bertani family—a child who was as ill-behaved and ill-fed a six-year-old as the Hill knew, by the way—why this same boy was once again missing from amongst our number. (Such absences from a class, I should mention here, are not uncommon, and are not considered to be an especial lapse of discipline by St Peter's. Many families on the Hill are in occupations which will require the participation of younger family members at short notice— but nonetheless, I still thought it my duty to make sure that the child was not unwell or injured). My question was met with silence, so I repeated it. A second silence then ensued; however, this one was qualified by the sound of some distant <u>fracas</u> or other, the source of which seemed to lie somewhere out on my class-room's staircase. I quite naturally assumed that this noise was some other master's affair, since it was so clearly emanating from at least a floor below us; I could hear nailed boots, and a raised male voice, but neither of those sounds were ones that I felt required my immediate attention. And so—assuming that no further response to my initial question was going to be forth-coming—I quietly opened my dictation-book at the appropriate page.

I forget now what our text was, in that moment—but it was certainly during its first sentence that I became aware that what-ever <u>fracas</u> this was, it had definitely turned a corner, and was now mounting noisily in our direction. Heads began to shift, and crane. I rapped on my desk, to gather the class's attention—I cleared my throat—and began once again to recite my chosen sentence. The shouting and scuffling grew closer—I paused—and the school-room door burst suddenly open.

I say <u>burst</u>, but the word is hardly adequate. Rather, I should say, the door was <u>exploded</u>—and not with sparks, but with a shower of invective so vivid that even my rude Italian appre-hended the sense.

The class rose, in immediate uproar.

Then, through the doorway, there appeared a diminu-tive and squirming figure. Its entrance I might say was more a marionette's than a person's, since its bare feet danced some inches above the floor—and it was being delivered into our midst by a sternly and quite horizontally extended fist and forearm, with the fingers of that same fist seemingly entwined in both the puppet's collar and its hair. The puppet was protesting vigorously at this treatment, and its face was quite the picture. The puppeteer, however, was still as yet unseen—but now, quite slowly, that fist and forearm were followed by the rest of the relevant limb—by a heaving-open jacket, which revealed a curl-strewn chest—and finally by a neck, collar and face. Mysteriously, the leggings, trousers and boots that also now became visible beneath this torso were almost entirely white; I assumed at the time they had been dusted with a kind of flour. Cursing all the while, and half-breathless with the task of keeping his mannikin aloft in such an extreme manner, the puppet-master then proceeded to carry his protesting burden down the central aisle of the room. As he did so, he delivered himself of a long and clearly heartfelt speech, one hissed mostly between clenched teeth—and most liberally peppered with imprecations.

The speech started with profuse apologies for the burden's lack of respect for the <u>Maestro Inglese</u>—<u>Madonna!</u> (here, a flailing puppet-foot found its target, and thus explained the precautionary extension of the puppeteer's arm)—and then went on to explain that the Signor Bertani—<u>Madonna!</u>—who lodges down on the Warner Street—<u>Madonna!</u>—this Signor Bertani had been obliged to request that he—<u>io stesso</u>—the owner of the arm and fist—might deliver to the school today this infant miscreant—<u>quest' baloche!</u>—on account of the said Signor Bertani not being able to deliver the child in person—<u>Madonna!</u>—as he had for once found work. And that the child had been already beaten—<u>naturalmente</u>—but should the <u>Maestro</u> feel it necessary to repeat the dose—<u>Sapristi!!</u>—

   And so on.

In my confusion, I could do nothing but watch—and, I fear, open-mouthed. Then, as if to rescue me from my immobility, the puppet-master took decisive action. Having reached the front of the class, he gathered his strength, engaged his spare hand in the puppet's breeches—and hoisted him so high into the air that the child squealed like a frightened pig. Then—as if to curtail this noise—the puppet-master simply dropped the boy (or so it seemed) straight down into an empty chair. The puppet emitted one last and solitary sob of shock—and the class too fell silent as it witnessed this feat of dexterity. The intruder reached down— briefly wiped his hands—and tugged the puppet up into a more respectfully attentive position. He then slapped it twice around the back of the head for good measure—but not vindictively, I noticed, rather with some care, and not a little amusement. Then, and only then, did my floury guest introduce himself. He stooped to collect his dropped cap, knocked back his tousled hair, shook himself like a dog, tucked the rolled cap into one of his armpits—vigorously wiped the palms of both his hands on his trousers again—extended his right hand—and told me his name.

   <u>M'scusi, Maestro; mi chiamo Michaele</u>, he said.

Then, since I did not answer, he translated for my benefit; <u>Maestro,</u> he said—shaping his lips very carefully, this time—<u>I am named Michaele.</u>

You have heard, I am sure, the expression 'my heart stopped'? Well, it did. That curling hair—those eyes—and now that Archangelic name! And yet, by what other could such a face have been christened? Oh, I may have told myself when I gave up my Vocation that I no longer believed in such air-borne carriers of grace—not even in the marvellously-painted forms they had been given by my beloved Masters—but trust me, as I beheld those darkened eyes, and parted lips, I knew straightway what quality of Divine Messenger now stood before my desk. For He had arrived exactly as angels are said to; He was Unexpected, yet Long-Desired. As soon as the first blunt shock of His beauty had subsided, and the breath had returned to my body, I recognised Michaele for what he truly was; my Heart's Desire, sent to me from Heaven, and made, miraculously—Flesh.

I shook the proffered hand, and thanked him. Then, I must confess, I stood and watched entranced again as he transferred that still-rolled cap to the other hand—for Oh, the grace of that gesture! He delivered a final parting slap to the back of the Bertani child's head, and then—with as little apology in the movements of his Departure as there had been in those of his sudden Arrival—he turned and walked away from me. I half-expected to witness some last great furling-up of plumage, as he went—but no; the boy simply closed the wooden door behind him.

I have no idea of how I continued that day's lesson. Or how I quelled the laughter which I only just now realised was leaping joyfully from my infant charges' throats, making our walls nearly shake.

§

St Peter's rings again. The bell of our <u>campanile</u> is cast not from iron, the people say, but from pure steel—<u>il ver' acciaio</u>—and it is that harshest of all metals that now instructs me to make haste. I have one fewer half-hour left, the bell tells me, in which to compose myself. One fewer half-hour before I next must face those pitch-dark eyes, that wine-dark mass of curls—that smiling, opening mouth.

§

In the evening, Fr. Ferrari sent a child-messenger to summon me back to the school. My mind was still disturbed—how could it not be?—and when this summons first came I confess I was somewhat alarmed. The Father gives a rudimentary English class for working-men and women on some evenings of the week—a class which employs a Magic Lantern display and the offer of well-sweetened tea to attract its attendance—and I imagined that his calling me back to Herbal Hill after this same late class could only be for some admonition. Possibly, one concerning the manner in which the truant Bertani child had been delivered to my classroom. I was also, I will admit, somewhat annoyed. I was eager that evening to keep to my room, and to relish the chance that its relative seclusion gave me to revisit and catalogue my thoughts.

When Fr Ferrari explained what he in fact wished to see me about, his words only added to my disturbed state of mind. As soon as he mentioned painting, I shrank—and regretted at once my boastfulness during that first February interview. I had, I said, no desire to revisit my early days of artistic ambition; I also said—and truly—that I had not picked up a pencil or attempted a composition for some fair few years. However, Fr Ferrari—canny old man that he is, fierce always in the cause of his establishment—brushed aside my objections with one brief wave of his hand. He explained—and with some emphasis—that perhaps as a newcomer— a <u>nuov'venuto</u>—I was unaware that the Hill was soon approaching the day of its annual procession or <u>Sagra,</u> a festival whose highlight would once again this year be the moment when Our Blessed Lady is carried in effigy down the marble steps of St Peter's church and then out and around the Hill to greet and bless her people. It was, he said, a most solemn and beautiful point of the year, one to which the entire <u>quartiere</u> looked forward—and then he came to his point. After some deliberation, the Board of St Peter's School had decided to commission a new banner for this year's procession. It was time, the gentlemen of the Board considered, that Our Lady should be joined on her journey by an attendant Saint. The cost of a painted figure on a banner had been discussed, Fr Ferrari said—the school was not by any means a rich one, as I was doubtless aware—and it had in fact been his own happy inspiration to remember that one of his Junior Masters might be just the person to undertake such a task, and quite possibly without charging a penny for his labour. Surely someone who had made such extensive study of these matters as myself might devise and execute such a simple thing as the figure of a Saint, on a mere canvas banner? A Junior Master like myself—the Board felt—as did the Father himself—would not want to let such an opportunity to serve both his school and Our Lady pass by. Would he?

Seeking some time in which to compose my answer, I enquired as to which particular Saint the Board was thinking of. Ah, said Fr Ferrari, we were thinking not of St Peter, but of Michael, the Prince of All Angels—he whose iron-tipped lance and shield signify the divine defeat of that Devil, Ignorance. Appropriate, did I not think? To express the salutations of a school?

A pair of black eyes blazed at once through my mind, and tangled all possible answers.

Recovered, I told Fr Ferrari that I would consider his request—and then muttered something about how a life-size figure of a saint on a banner would however be a challenge to any artist, trained or not. Fr Ferrari rapped his desk and said, well would I please give him my answer soon, since the procession left the Church on the third Sunday in July, and it was now almost the middle of June. As he was sure I was aware.

§

A life-sized figure of a Saint—how on earth was I to achieve such a thing? I had never been trained in a Life Room! That night, my first mental attempts at sketching a well-armoured torso not unnaturally brought my thoughts back to our class-room—to the outstretched arm and curl-decked breast of that Appearing Angel—and it was then, with his figure coming in and out of focus in my imagination, that I realised that my first stunned encounter with the boy had left me with no information about him beyond the bare fact of his Christian name. I knew no address, for instance; so how was I ever, therefore, to witness his Beauty again? Immediately, I imagined myself pacing the Hill's steep streets, replacing my mutterings of Dante with some de-ranged plea to Heaven that it might make its Messenger appear to me once more. This image of myself made me laugh—but only bitterly. These first imaginings then mingled themselves with others—with images of things I had seen elsewhere on the Hill. Bright shawls, flung back from scornful eyes; men whose shoulders and arms had been blackened and polished by work. I recalled an alleyway paved with the glitter of discarded ice—and how a cluster of men there had watched me as I slid and almost fell. I put these fragments together—a glance of contempt here, a finely carved neck below—and wondered how they would look all framed by some splendid suit of antique armour. I gave my assemblage a pair of black eyes, and a wealth of tousled hair. I composed until I fell asleep—and then fell even further, right back to a Vestry floor.

§

On Sunday, I awoke with the six o'clock bell—and with a thought as clear as my dreams had been dark. Surely, the boy would attend a Mass—the whole Hill attends, and St Peter's church is busy fully half the day with accommodating its crowds. All I had to do was to choose my spot, and then wait. I was used already to attending <u>one</u> of these Sunday Masses—that was a duty expected of us school-masters—and so the only question now was how I might discreetly attend the entire sequence. I had, after all, no idea as to which of the day's services the boy himself would choose to join, and I did not want to invite attention by becoming too conspicuous a loiterer. I decided that a simple but regular shifting of my vantage point within the church would suffice. The equally simple story of a necessary visit to some fictional friend served to excuse me from joining Sra Galleatti and her family for my usual Sunday dinner; I invented for this friend an address somewhere over on the Hackney Downs, I remember, a place I have never visited in my life, but whose name I knew from the sign-boards of Omnibuses—and then, as the steel bell tolled for the first Mass of the day, I brushed my hair, hurried past my four usual corners, and mounted the white marble steps of St Peter's with my hat in my hand.

The church felt full of eyes—and I, a fraud. My lips moved when required to, for I remembered my responses; however, those lips of mine could just as easily have cursed, as murmured, for my desired quarry was nowhere to be seen. At one Office, I recall, there was a knot of Irishmen standing amongst all the Italian Catholics; one young man of their number seemed to have hair made only of angry, upstanding flames. He was a Beauty—but not the one I sought. As I stared at him, I heard distant voices—my mind ran in strange channels of memory—and my thoughts returned me to places I had no wish now to revisit. Back in Birmingham, I had used sometimes to weep during Holy Office, and can even remember retching at the altar-rail itself. There were long hours of humiliation, then—of prayers spoken only to the empty air—and it was not pleasant to feel the old bile of Despair rising once more towards my throat. I thought my eyes might bleed, with all the watching—and the boy never came.

That night, my thoughts as I lay sleepless in this narrow coffin of a bed-room were full—and again, they were dark. But if in future years you are judging me, please do remember in what a bitter School of Life I had been trained. Remember also how long I had kept that sacred Vow of mine; how many days—and nights...

If you can, be kind to my memory.

A second long Sunday proved as fruitless as the first; this time, I recall, I even gave my imaginary friend out on the Hackney Downs a name—and as I did so, became half-frightened at how an adept a purveyor of untruths I had now become.

But never to myself did I lie. No; never to myself.

§

It was, I think, less than a week later when I found myself halfway up the pavement of Great Sutton Street. It was my dinner-time, and presumably I was out there at the furthest edges of the Hill in order to purchase some small domestic item on behalf of Sra Galleatti—but who knows, for my mind was wandering as surely as my footsteps. I remember shadows, and sunlight on the opposite pavement—the sound of a barrel-organ, and my feet being about to cross the street—when there, suddenly, and in a darkened doorway, stood the boy. He was scowling, as if against some unwonted brightness; his shirt-sleeves were rolled high onto the muscles of his arms—there was no strained-open jacket to frame his breast, this time—and the shabby boots and trousers down below were once again all caked in flour-like dust. Even his hyacinthine curls wore a coating of this powder now—and his face itself was entirely white. Truly, his features seemed to be some livid-eyed statue's, and they quite frightened me. Michaele was smoking—pinching the inverted cigarette between his first finger and thumb, like all the men and boys do here—and when he lifted this tobacco back up to his lips, our eyes met.

Desire—True Desire—makes all the senses sharp. People may talk of needles, and of haystacks, but let me tell you; such similes are inexact. To lovers, metal of the piercing kind has a distinctively different shine to that of straw, and the two could not ever be confused. What I was looking at across the width of Great Sutton Street is something that enters in through the eyes, then reaches its target in one dreadful and simple stroke. Believe me; I have felt that deadly operation.

The boy seemed unsure at first who it was, that was staring at him so strangely. The day was warm, and my schoolmaster's coat lay over my arm—but then, when I waved in tentative greeting, he grinned in recognition. I left my vantage point, smiling now in reply—and as I stepped down across the curb-way, my feet began to tangle, exactly like those of that puppet in my school-room. Indeed, looking back, it is a wonder that I did not actually fall! Michaele flicked his cigarette away quickly—smiled at my stumbling—and quickly wiped his hands on his trousers as he came out into the street to catch me. The blackness of his eyes seemed to burn even brighter, as I felt his hand support my arm. They were as sloes, sliced with a silver knife; holes, burnt in some ancient tapestry by a pair of smoking torches.

I have no proper recollection of what Italian phrases or words were then delivered or exchanged between us, but I am sure our conversation was ordinary. I do remember laughter, and the boy telling me with many gestures that this was where he did his work, making the little plaster statues of the saints to be coloured and painted in the back of Sr Pagliai's workshop here (that was the name painted up on the board above the window, I noted). Now at last I understood the white dust—that it was Plaster of Paris, I mean—and I imagined, hearing his explanations, and watching him so laughingly pantomime his daily routine (of course, I did not say this) that it was perhaps his frequent hefting of great sacks of the stuff that had gifted him his remark-able figure. I made shift with my Italian as best I could, by way of some response, but the conversation between us dried like a stream in summer. Michaele shook himself—apologised for the new cloud of whiteness that this action released—and then indicated by way of a pair of open palms and an eye-roll that he was overdue at his work. He disappeared back into the darkness of the shop's doorway, and all the company of saints arranged there in its shop-window seemed suddenly quite lifeless. Also, all of them—I thought—seemed to be suddenly frowning.

It was only once he was fully vanished that I realised I had once again asked Michaele nothing of value; not his family name, for instance, and certainly not where or with whom he might be found living. I had done nothing but grin, and make I am sure the most basic of grammatical errors. However, I *had* mentally noted the address of Sr Pagliai's statue-workshop—and that, I suppose, was the beginning of my plan. I would go to Fr. Ferrari—I decided, that evening—and announce that I had found on Great Sutton Street a possible model for this painting of his Saint. A model who seemed to be working at a business which I felt sure that he—the Father—must know. If he expressed surprise at the thought of such a boy serving as my inspiration—a boy hailing from the (shall we say) meaner streets of the city—then I would speak warmly of Michaele's potentially military bearing—of his noble chest, and head—and—even better—I would speak of the boy's Christian name. That was it! Father, I would say, the boy is almost an Archangel already. Surely such a Coincidence may be taken as a Sign?

§

When I left that Chemist's in Birmingham, I did so in a fury—I had been accused of impertinence to a male customer, and dismissed without reference. And so, before leaving, and in lieu of the missing wages to which I felt myself entitled, I had helped myself to a still-boxed Sanderson camera from the top shelf of my employer's stock-room. I felt no qualms at taking such an expensive thing, for I felt myself the wronged party—and, despite the camera's value, this same stubborn instinct of Justification had then made me keep it close by me throughout all my subsequent wanderings. Even during my worst days of hunger, I had never pawned it—and when the time came for me to shift to London, I duly packed it in the bottom of my suitcase. Once I returned home after my encounter with Michaele on Great Sutton Street, I reached beneath my bed—and it was this same battered suitcase that my fingers were then seeking.

Thank God, everything seemed to be still in working order.

Then, the very next night, and merely perhaps to distract myself from my still-whirling thoughts—although again, I must ask myself if there was not some Providence in this coincidence also—I stayed late in my schoolroom, studying an Italian Vocabulary. This work done—or rather, abandoned—I then went downstairs, and came across Fr Ferrari giving that adult evening class of his. The lantern-slides were all of Italy, that night, and as I sipped my tea, and watched the crudely-outlined colours come and go across the school-hall plaster, my plan took a further turn. I saw Etna smoke Yellow, and the Forum of Rome glow Crimson, and as their paint-box boldness came and went on the walls I suddenly realised how I might proceed.

Well; the imagination has its own dark chemistry, does it not?

In that Birmingham back-room, you see, one of my commonest tasks had been the turning of glass negatives into slides for lantern-projection. This is a process which the Customers seemed to find mysterious or even magical, but in fact it is mostly a question of due care and attention when mixing one's solutions. And now, here—on a scrubbed school wall, in Clerkenwell—Fr Ferrari's display had shown me just how easily I might capture the very body of my Saint. Michaele would sit for me as a photographic study; the Sanderson would expose and record him; a careful washing with some salts would change the glass of the plate into that of a slide; the lantern would project that slide onto a canvas banner, hung on the school-hall wall, and then I—well I will not say <u>hey presto</u>, though I am sure I felt the phrase—I, with some charcoal and brushes, would then trace his figure upon that banner—trace it, to the Life! The final colouring-in—the covering of the boy's limbs with armour, for instance—the adding of wings and a lance, together with some lurking serpent or other, to represent his vanquished Adversary—all of these things could be contrived afterwards. A suitably Satanic reptile could be easily enlarged from an illustrated work of Natural History; the armour and wings could be taken from a Signorelli altarpiece that I already knew by heart. My mind moved fast; the branch of Kodak Limited that stood up on the corner of Turnmills, I decided, could probably most reasonably provide me with all the necessary chemicals; however, the supply of Ilford's Art Paper that I was going to need for my testing-session prints would probably have to be purchased from further afield. It wasn't the cheapest of papers, as I remembered, but it was certainly the very best for capturing the subtler shades of skin, and hair. I would find it somewhere on Oxford Street, without a doubt.

There were only two stumbling blocks.

First, I would need the services of a dark-room. Here, I thought briefly of using commercial premises—of taking my plates to a local Chemist's to be developed, in other words—but the thought of some back-room amateur sniggering over images of Michaele was at once abhorrent. Then I looked around me. This very room—this stifling one-person prison of a bed-room, divided from Sra Galleatti's front room by only its one, thinly-plastered wall—well it was surely all I needed! The door had a lock already, and an hour spent with some glue and scissors—with some ochre-tinted paper, cut to fit the panes of my window—and I would surely have quite soon contrived the distinctively bloody gloom that my task would require. True, getting my landlady's consent for such a use of my room might be delicate—she might well have concerns about the proximity of the necessary chemicals to the two children, I thought, once I started the actual work of development—but I trusted that some early mention of Fr Ferrari's role in the business would soon ease her mind. She might even lend me some of her white china soup-plates, I thought, for the bathing and fixing.

All of this was good; however, I was still left with my second obstacle. Where was I to take my photographs in the first place? As any Photographer will tell you, the initial fixing of the image requires considerable light, just as the later processes require a dense but manageable darkness. In addition, I anticipated that my work might require some Privacy. A room in the school, perhaps? Too busy—and like all of the buildings on Herbal Hill, St Peter's was too hemmed-in; too light-denied, as blind Milton once put it...

Well, the school and its street may be dark—but The Buildings here are not. Their six stories rise well above the roofs of our older neighbours, and in consequence of this Sra Galleatti's living-room basks in that rarest of all London luxuries; unimpeded daylight. The room is not by any means large, of course—the table and the children's cots fill it almost completely, making our meal-times a matter all of clashing knees and elbows—but it is well lit; the window faces south, and the Signora keeps its glass as spot-less as the china of her table. I calculated swiftly; by shifting the table back against the left-hand wall, and getting the boy up on top of it, there would be just distance enough for me to capture the full-length figure I needed. Not to mention the right upwards perspective, for a Saint intended to be carried above peoples' heads.

Here too, I worried about how to broach such a strange use of her premises to Sra Galleatti—but my worries proved needless. When at my instigation Fr Ferrari came round the next evening, to put my project to her in person, there was little need for negotiation of any kind. Indeed, once she understood that the final fruit of my labours was to be a banner waving in the sunshine of the coming <u>sagra</u>, my landlady said that she would not only happily lend her Living-room to be my Studio, but would surely stitch and press the canvas of the banner herself. <u>It will make the Virgin smile on my house and boys</u>, she said—and crossed herself.

You see? Everything conspired to bring us together—everything! I was to go to the earliest of that Sunday's Masses, and Sra Galleatti was to take the children out to the one at ten o'clock. Sr Galleatti, as always, would have business of his own on a Sunday morning, and Sr Pagliai—who of course *was* known to Fr Ferrari, as I had guessed, because four of his workshop's little plaster saints kept watch on the staircase of St Peter's Parish Office—Sr Pagliai was to instruct his employee to knock on Sra Galleatti's front door at ten o'clock exactly. I was then to have the boy for an entire—and uninterrupted—hour.

I smiled.

I was absolutely sure that an hour would be plenty, you see. I was also—and this is indeed strange, looking back—absolutely calm, as I heard all of my contrivance being so easily agreed-to by these strangers.

§

He wore his Sunday suit—and had combed his hair down flat.

He looked rather younger, now that he was clean, and indeed when I enquired after his age, I was surprised to be told by Michaele that he was fully one month past seventeen. Work, I suppose, always does make a boy seem older, and it was only in his working-clothes (and dirt) that I had hitherto seen him. I enquired after that work, to be polite—we spoke in Italian, as before—and Michaele treated me again to his pantomime of sack-heaving. Then, we set to. First, I explained to him in as simple terms as I could what our hour together was going to entail. I stumbled over some of the more technical words, necessarily—and I could see that the boy was looking around, evidently wondering how on earth our task was to be accomplished in such cramped and domestic surroundings—and so to reassure him, I showed him some of the rough sketches I had made earlier, of the Saint's military pose, and so on—and indicated how the figure would only be equipped at the very final stage of our collaboration with wings and an adversary. Questo—il Diavolo? he asked, pointing to the roughly coiled lines at the bottom of my sketch, the one's beneath the Saint's feet, and Yes, I said; Yes, Michaele; that will be the very Devil Himself. I explained that this first sitting of ours was to be by way of an experiment—for the light and the exposures, I said, as it had been some time since I had last done any of this—and then I asked him to take his jacket off. Which he did with good grace. I then went to quite some trouble to explain again how still he must keep for me, and that I would indicate each of the poses he was to adopt for me in turn. He nodded, slicked back his hair, and seemed easy.

These boys of the Hill—they are used to being stared at. It is they, not the women, who are the true peacocks of this place, for all their often-scowling looks.

I took my own jacket off also—for ease of movement—and then we started our session. Michaele did well; he let me angle him away from or into the light from the window just as I required, and showed no sign of hesitation whenever I asked him to lower his gaze or sit slightly forward at the table. For this first session, I concentrated just on his face, hair, hands and upper body, testing all of my distances and exposures very carefully as I went. After all—as I said—it had been some time since I had done any of this, and I wanted to allow for any possible clumsiness on my part. I was very careful not to ever have Michaele face into the camera directly, I might say, and thus avoided the possibility of any direct assault or distraction from his eyes. Our allotted hour passed quickly, and the boy was easily gone and the dining-table returned to its proper place by the time the family came home for their meal.

§

It is a curious thing to spend an hour with your Heart's Desire, and for him to laugh, and smile, and co-operate, and yet for him to know nothing of what you are truly thinking. But trust me, that first strangeness is as nothing compared to the later oddity of realising—as you stand leaning on the dark side of a now-shut front door, and listening to his footsteps as they retreat down flights of stairs—that you have not quite breathed or spoken freely for the whole of the sixty minutes. And—trust me, again—that second and day-lit strangeness is once again less than nothing compared to the dismay that is set to rise and smite you after the family that you live with have returned laughingly home from their allotted Mass, and you have sat and eaten your Sunday meal with them—your heart still half-thumping in your chest, all the while—and you have then retreated to your room, and closed the door and locked it, and started your work of darkness with hopeful and shaking hands...

It was dreadful; my test-studies, as they emerged from the soup-plates, were a disaster. The boy's skin looked as lifeless as if it had been still plastered with that dreadful dust of his—his hands, thick-fingered—and his hair seemed one single slab of ordinary and undifferentiated blackness. Even I could not see his beauty. I think I had imagined, while I was working, that the ardency of my vision would manifest itself quite automatically. However—as I now discovered—the exact opposite had occurred. My feelings had made my eye both dull, and dulling. In addition, I seemed to have badly miscalculated my exposures, for my tones were as dim as my model seemed commonplace.

As I looked at what I had done, I remembered other faces; other faces, that had also turned ordinary in the bald light of day. Then, I gathered myself, and committed the necessary murder. Adding an excess of hydrochloric to the developing solution, I watched as oblivion crept slowly across the glass of my exposed plates. Once inky, they snapped between my fingers like the Host.

§

Unwilling to admit defeat, I told myself that the problem was not my eye, but the lighting of my improvised Studio. The day, after all, had been a slightly cloudy one. I mentioned this impediment to Sra Galleatti, who was of course eager to know how my project had progressed—and it was she who suggested the solution. The bundled-up tablecloths and napkins which she had brought home with her the previous evening were Soho ones, she told me, belonging to the restaurant of a Galleatti cousin; laundering them was one of her few regular jobs, as it happened, and this lot need not be returned for a week. By the time she and I had un-crumpled half a dozen, and then hung the dining-room with their whiteness, the light in my makeshift studio was much corrected. Indeed, my heart leapt, when I stood back and surveyed our handiwork, for the space where the boy would eventually be standing on the table now seemed lifted to another and almost pristine world. Then, as if to approve our labours, a cloud shifted somewhere outside the window—and the whole room dazzled. The Signora clapped her hands, and the boys both laughed out loud.

§

On our second Sunday, I asked Michaele immediately to remove his jacket, and then also to go to the kitchen faucet and straightaway wash that flattening oil from out of his hair. I explained that we were going to do everything from the last session again, at which he seemed somewhat surprised—but nonetheless, he did as he was told, and we soon set efficiently back to work. I sat him to one side of the table—the light was good—and the sun came out to favour us again. The linen did its appointed work, and quite quickly my model began to look a little more like his true self. I exposed half my first packet of plates on his face and hands alone, and then—emboldened—I got him standing on the table. A Saint must look down on the world, I explained, and then I went to the hall-cupboard, and produced the broom-handle that was to be our substitute lance; I also lifted a pillow from my bed, to stand in for the trampled serpent. Stand like a soldier for me now, I told Michaele—un'soldato, Michaele—un'Militario, I said, indicating that I wanted his back straight, his chin up and his hands held rigid by his side—as if he was carrying the lance on a drill-parade, I explained, and was Standing At Attention. Again, he did as he was told quite promptly. I had the table between me and the window still, at this point, and so my Saint was now all silhouetted; to correct this, I moved the camera round, and the table back against the far wall, and thus contrived to get all of him within my sights and properly lit. This was much better, and I felt not a little excitement. Then, my Saint—unbidden, it must be said—began to play for me up there on his makeshift pedestal; he broke the stiffness of the lines that I had given him, and lifted his broom-handle high. Smiling all the while to himself, he began driving its shaft down and down again into the serpent-pillow under his feet—and because the day was warm by now, and the sun rather strong, his shirt began to cling to him quite closely. I began to see the true shape of his body, emerging very clearly into the light—the two beautifully moulded discs or shields that made up his chest, for instance, and the flange of muscle up there under his arm, the one that was repeatedly bunching and flexing as the Saint drove his broom-handle home—and suddenly, Stay still! I shouted, Stay still and do not move one jot, Michaele—because those muscles are just what I need, I suddenly thought; they are just what I need to make the crowd believe that this Angel has wings indeed—just what we need to make our Saint take flight! Michaele started laughing, then—and I suppose it was the effort with the lance that was making him vent his breath so—or perhaps he was laughing at some new note of enthusiasm in my usually schoolmasterly voice—I cannot quite say—but anyway, tossing back his now-curling hair, the boy asked me E questo che t'vuoi, Padrone—not using the word Maestro to me now, as before, but this new word—one that I barely noticed, in my excitement—and so, Yes, Michaele—I said—that is exactly what I want—really only half-hearing the word he had used, you see, in my haste and enthusiasm—Oh yes exactly—please do not move one inch! And at that, he lifted the broom-handle once more—as if it really was steel-tipped, this time—and seemed all at once to somehow quite completely hold his breath, so that he really did make himself into some sort of a statue up there on our make-shift table-plinth, even with his one arm flung suddenly out like that and his lance so wonderfully aimed. Astonished, I hastily prepared a plate—working as quickly as I dared, lest my Saint should lose this marvellous pose—but my fingers fumbled, and the glass broke. At that, Michaele let fall a sound that should have been a laugh, but wasn't. He relaxed his arm, lifted the neck of his shirt so that it opened, and proceeded to blow calmly down beneath it, making the map of sweat that had been printed across the front of the fabric shift, and swell. Then, he swore to himself—using a word I really didn't catch, this time—and then, when he had done all of that, he quite deliberately shifted his gaze. His eyes were aimed now not at the camera, but at me; they darkened, and focussed; they sought—and found. At this, the very air of the room seemed to quail; it became somehow thick, and quite entirely still. Watching me fumble with a second plate, Michaele slowly lifted his lance again—and then, in the sudden thickness and stillness of the room's air, he used the word again. Its three syllables dropped softly from his lips; but all the steel of St Peter's bell lay beneath that softness. And this time, the word was very definitely a question.

I should explain. The word <u>padrone</u> comes from the old country, and it is used here on the Hill with only a very dark and particular sense—Fr Ferrari, for instance, will not have it spoken in his presence. The men only use it when they think no stranger can hear, for they consider that to be a <u>padrone</u> gives one man the right to use another entirely; I mean, to use his body as that of a slave, if required, or even of a beast. Michaele had kept his eyes fully on mine as he spoke this dark word for the second time—

his chest was rising, and falling—and the light was carving his figura very sharply. His shirt had fallen right open, now—and now, without wavering in his gaze, he offered the word to me for a third and final time. As he did so, his eyes were all black, insolent fire.

And that was when I heard the laughter. It was the family—Sr and Sra Galleatti and the children—returning from St Peter's for their Sunday meal. The children shrieked, seeing a man half-dressed and standing on their dinner-table, but Sra Galleatti sent them away with a clap of her hands to wash, and said she was sorry to disturb, but might she? The table? Michaele was already clambering down and tugging his shirt closed, and as he helped her lift the table back into its usual place she asked him if he would stay and take his meal with all the family—she was sure next door would lend a chair, she said, and the cooking would easily stretch—but no, he said—Grazie Signorina, ma no—and shrugged his jacket back on as if these Sunday clothes and manners were his usual ones, and as if the preceding minutes had never happened. As if I had imagined them, entirely.

After all, I had achieved no exposure of the boy's final pose; I had secured no proof of what Michaele intended by that word, and if he chose to now deny it…

At the front door, I thanked him for his time, and he laughed again—sideways—and said he would surely come again and finish the job if the Father instructed him to, for the Church—and then he crossed himself and was gone. I listened to him whistling something as he went away down the stairs—Rossini,

I think it was—and then went back inside. I cleared away my camera, helped pull down the tablecloths, and ate my meal without tasting it. Then I excused myself, and took myself away.

I had thought of taking my cares into the quiet of St Peter's— the Masses would soon be done, and a church seemed as good a place as any to try and hide my racing thoughts—but the thought of the squat confessionals there—of their questions—drove me straight past the church's marble steps. I walked I know not where—through streets, and squares, and alleyways. A coaxing voice called out after me at one point, but I didn't turn my head. I was wrestling with an Angel already—and indeed, with my Self. I knew I had not mistaken the boy's intentions; I knew that there were other trades besides those in ice and plaster, on the Hill— and that I was a schoolmaster, and he an ill-paid boy. I knew that if his eyes had been frank, then mine had surely betrayed me.

I walked until dark. Then, when I got home, I washed my face, shut my bedroom door, and got out my Drawing-Board. After that last session, you see, I felt the need to start again. Before I drew, I carefully shuttered my eyes. Before this night is over, I told myself, I must wipe my mind quite clear of Michaele's suggestion. I must clear it—focus it—and transform what I had seen looking down at me from Sra Galleatti's table back into a thing of Purity and Holy Beauty.

It took some work—much more than one hour's—but eventually, with some adjustments, I was able to revise my Saint's pose entirely. Remembering those last moments, I drew him poised, and raised up on the ball of one foot; with his free arm now thrown out, and his lance aloft. I also kept the Saint's face looking straight out towards the camera, whereas before I had kept it modestly—and prudently—down-turned. Working late into the night, I made my Archangel now wield his lance as he should. Stroke by stroke, and touch by touch, I made him into something air-borne, and wind-washed, and noble.

In the early hours—of course—my fingers began to cramp. However, although there were details still to resolve—the exact dimensions of the shield, for instance—the breadth of the wings, and the pose of the crouching Devil—I felt that my vision of the Saint's body itself was complete. When this morning is fully light—I told myself—I will go to the school, and I shall speak to Fr Ferrari again. The boy is a more than capable model, I shall say, and he takes his poses well; however, in order to do full honour to our Saint, I feel that he and I must endure one final extra session together. Also, Father—I shall say—as I am sure I do not really need to remind you, even after the glass plates are all taken and fixed, I will still have all the tracing of the figure from the lantern-slide to the canvas to achieve—the painting, and the gilding with all the colours—and the time is now really rather short. Really, Father, it is almost a crisis—I shall say—and I must insist that you release me from the school for an entire afternoon this week, and persuade Sr Pagliai to give me the boy for that same afternoon also. For this vision of a Winged and Armèd Victory is one that must be fully achieved—I shall say—or not achieved at all. Perhaps on this coming Thursday?

It worked. Today is Thursday, and I am being released from school at the two o'clock bell. Miss Deacon is to take my classes for me, and Michaele is to be released from work—I understand Sr Pagliai has been spoken to, and everything agreed. Sra Galleatti has made arrangements to be elsewhere with the children, and I am to have the key to her front door in my pocket. I am to have my model for three full and private hours this time, and Fr Ferrari says that the boy has been instructed to oblige me in every respect. Michaele understands, Fr Ferrari says, what will be required of him, and that this will be our very last chance to get things right between us.

§

The sun went down red last night, turning the windows here all bloody—and now—listen—the tide of noise on the Clerkenwell Road is rising steadily. The brewery carts across the way are already on the move.

What am I thinking of, do I hear you enquire across the years? What am I thinking of, as I lie here on this narrow bed of mine?

I am thinking of how all the places and faces of a tale connect, and how they may resolve themselves at the last into one fully rewarding composition; I am thinking of how, when you submit a photographic figure-study to its final bath, the salts eat away at all that is unnecessary, leaving only the Essential.

I am thinking that once an image is fixed, the body in that

image cannot ever then change.

But what will you do if the boy offers himself up to you again, I hear you ask—if he offers himself up again as he did that last time, when he stood above you on your table? The question is a valid one, not least since I have decided that it may be better for Michaele to work in his under-linen for me today, the better for the camera to capture the lineaments of this new and demanding pose. And if I do require him to do that—even if I busy myself with my cloths and plates, at the requisite moment—surely my eyes will lift and wander, as my Archangel begins to unbutton before me? And then, if he rises, and stands, and shows himself to me full-length up there on the dining-table—if he turns that fiery gaze once more upon me, and raises his lance to strike— what will become of me then? Most especially, what will become of my vow?

I think I have found a way to keep it.

This is what I see; I see young men—and women—lifting their eyes to gaze. I see every door on the Hill left open, and every street made riotous with flowers; I see old women laughing and clapping their hands together as my finally-finished banner comes swaying round the corners of the Clerkenwell sagra; I see it swaying left, and right, and left again, as the raucous music thrills the assembled crowd. Then, I see old hands flicking—as Sra Galleatti does, to blind the Devil when the salt gets spilt; I see knotted fingers crossing themselves, as their owners realise what my banner shows. And believe me, they will have reason, for when I have finished this work of mine my Saint will not be solitary—oh no; his feet will rest on a Devil such as these crooked streets have never seen. He will be a Brute, my chosen serpent— un Ver' Diavolo—a great nightmare knot of scales, topped by a blunt and searching head... The library book where I found his model yesterday shows the beast still sleeping—but I can easily wake him, with my charcoal wand! I can make his flesh open up like a flower—like a flower, or fissure—like a mouth, to receive that steel-tipped lance. I can make the thick coils of his body rise up around that penetrating blade, and greet it almost with a woman's rapture. Oh, my Diavolo shall be proud to serve as a pedestal—and as the crowds lift their eyes—and applaud—and cross themselves—this creature's half-familiar features will gaze steadily up to Heaven, even as its head tips back and falls—falls back, in that longed-for and extinguishing Agony of which I believe we all so fiercely dream. And when I have finished with my work, the scarlet of this beast's tongue will indeed flicker and flame, as he dies—but not with Despair. His eyes will widen— but not with Despair! They shall be my eyes—mine—and it will be in an agony of Love that they shall blaze; it shall be to Love alone that they bear their lofty witness.

I speak not for living ears; I speak to those who will come after me.

As the bell now tolls, in this year of 1891, I imagine my boy's boots, predicting him on the stairs. I see him raising his hand to knock; I see him using our black-painted door as a mirror, and running his fingers through that always-miraculous hair. I see his smile—his smile!—and now I hear my own voice, calling out to him through that still-shut door, saying unto him Come in, my love; come in, and let us begin our great work together. Come in, for the door is now unlocked, and the day is surely breaking.

72 Seaton Point

D on't get me wrong; I love visiting the girls. I love going up there for my dinner sometimes. But 'The Downs'? Come on. Whoever was after choosing that for a suitable name? Sure there's the odd tree or two, from the council, but mostly the girls' address is nothing rural at all, just one big blasted-looking stretch of grass with concrete walkways going all across it and then the one big old tower-block sitting right in the middle of everything. The one that they *didn't* demolish, in the 90s. And then, when you've finally got yourself up there to the eighteenth floor, and you're thinking well at least there'll be a view—honestly, the only half-way proper line of trees you can see from out of that window there by the lift is all the way over on the top of Hampstead Heath.

Now where I grew up—that was what you'd call country. Just twenty minutes up from Dublin by the train, or forty in my Uncle Diarmaid's car, but those were proper hills that we had for a view there from the end of our street. Big enough for a boy to set his dreams in.

Actually, I'm going up to the girls' place for my dinner again tonight. And—actually—it's to be a dinner for all four of us.

Sweet Mary, did I ever imagine I'd be thinking *that* as sentence! I mean, not even this time last year, because this time last year, if I'd been greeting you at some do for work, at the library say, or if I was out and about on the town or whatever—and if I liked the look of you, and thought you were at least reasonably age-appropriate—I'd have been telling you, hello, my name is Jacky; I'm thirty-four, and I'm as single as they come. And now, tonight, just a year and whatever later, well tonight it's going to be four chairs set out around that table on the eighteenth floor, and four glasses set ready for the anniversary toast. It's going to be Shaz, and her Alex, plus me and my Jonah.

This time last year? That was the girls' big day out at the Hackney Town Hall.

§

We were supposed to be down at the Hall for half nine at the latest—the Registrar had been very insistent about us not missing our 10 a.m. slot, it being the very first one of the day—and so I'd booked the taxi for nine on the dot. Just to be on the safe side, you know? Except that now, it was easily nudging a quarter past. The driver downstairs was ringing me every five minutes to tell me he had another booking to get to—and Alex was still foosthering about with her tie-knot in front of the bathroom mirror. Shaz was out on the landing, madly pressing lift-buttons, safely in her dress alright—but without her flowers. And the lift wasn't coming—as per usual, in that block—so she was yelling back in through the open front door of the flat could somebody please get the carnations out of the bath while she kept on with the buttons, and *that* meant that Xardine—who was officially Matron of Honour for the day, and so was supposed to be in charge—well it meant that Xardine was actually beginning to lose it already. Hence the loud and not entirely ladylike sound of her shouting out through the open front door that no she couldn't fetch the effing flowers, because she was still trying to find Alex's effing front door keys. All of which meant that it was down to your man here to sort the flowers, while also explaining to the taxi driver that another three minutes should do it. Flowers delivered—*without* getting any water on the dress, which wasn't easy, I can tell you—I then checked my watch again and thought perhaps I'd better leave Alex to Xardine, and crack on with the final run-around myself, even though that hadn't been the plan. The final make-sure that we really were all set for everybody coming back afterwards, you know? Was the ice sorted, were the spare toilet-rolls where we'd agreed, was there juice for the kids. All that sort of thing.

Well, I could see that the ice was fine, all sitting in the kitchen sink with the first round of cans, and the finger-food on the living-room table was all properly draped over with tea-towels. I even checked that the little framed photograph was hanging straight on its nail there, the one that Alex had banged in over the gas fire just last night—but Mother of God, the place looked wrong.

It looked like we were all trying way too hard to make this

work, you see. It had that sort of Christmas morning look to it, when you've got the place all done up to the nines for the family, but you just know that things are going to go wrong later. And I suppose every Big Day has its nerves—and I suppose also, what with the civil partnerships having only become an actual and legal thing just a few months previous, this particular day was bound to have a fair few more than most—but I do remember very distinctly standing there in the girls' living-room with that picture staring down at me, and meanwhile hearing Xardine back in the bedroom shouting well where the fuck do you *think* you left them Alex, and feeling all of a sudden that nothing much in the room looked right at all. And if I'm honest, I think maybe what triggered it was your man up there in that photo.

Seeing him and his lady wife looking down at the way we'd got the table done, I reckon that was taking me back to Blackrock. If there was a wedding or First Communion due in Blackrock, you see—that being where I grew up—then it would have been my mother and her sisters laying out the food in the front parlour, and you can bet your life the tea-towels would all have had straight edges. Nobody would have been shouting after last-minute keys in *that* house. And remembering all of that, I was also after seeing the face of our priest Father O'Halloran coming up the front path again, who let me tell you I hadn't given a thought to for years. I was remembering when he came to the house that time, to shout at my mother. About me. I was after seeing his hair, and that mean twisting mouth he always had on him at confession.

I was after hearing some woman's voice, leaning in close to my ear during a wedding mass, whispering to me sure one day that'll be you up there at the altar-rail Jacky, making your mother proud.

Mrs O'Riordan, she was called, the owner of that voice; lived two doors down from us on O'Connell Street.

Had a son, who used to beat me after school.

So, yes, I was standing there, seeing and hearing all of that—seeing and hearing all of the exact things that had made me get on the Holyhead ferry aged eighteen, in other words—and I can tell you, they were very definitely making me need the day's first drink. But then, just as I was about to head back to the kitchen to open the one solitary bottle of Powers whiskey we'd got lined up on the worktop there, all of sudden Xardine—God bless her—Xardine shouted out that she'd finally found Alex's keys on the bedside cabinet, and would I just grab her own bag from off the sofa please, because apparently the effing lift was finally here. So I checked I'd got my notes for the speech—which would have been for the twentieth time that morning already, I reckon—and took myself a deep breath. Then, I shut my eyes for a second, and pressed the palm of my hand against the glass of the girls' big living-room window there. The glass up on the eighteenth floor stays icy even when the sun's out—at least in April it does—and I guess I just needed to feel that jolt of cold for a moment. Just to stiffen myself for what we were all about to do together. You know?

One year ago exactly. And as I say; if anyone had told me then…

§

The actual business of arriving and waiting at the Town Hall went fine, in the end, and I have to say that the Registrar was terrific when it came to the service itself. There was not one word of a stumble over it being two women in front of her for a change. Well, there was a *bit* of a moment, when she started referring to someone called Alessandra, and because so many of us had forgotten I think that Alessandra was actually Alex's real name, a couple of people passed comment. Apart from that, which I could see threw her a little, the woman kept a totally straight face on her. Even when the girls got to doing their vows—which let's be honest, must have been no mean feat.

Alex—God love her—had chosen to read the lyrics from an old Janis Joplin song. *Take another little piece of my heart*, you know? *Babe I'm going to show you, that a woman can be tough*—and so on. All of which certainly went with Alex's look for the day, which was a new suit and tie, plus short-back-and-sides, plus her very best stone-butch expression throughout; but still, I have to say, I never knew that Joplin song had *quite* so many words.

Shaz, meanwhile, was all in silver satin, all very thirties-style and cut low in the back, and when it got to her turn, well I don't know all the Shakespeare poems, but I did know this one. *Let me not to the marriage of true minds admit impediment.* And so on.

Which kind of stopped the show. For me, anyway, because the way she did them, those old words came out of Shaz's mouth like they'd been waiting just for this one particular day to finally make sense of themselves. Also, she managed to keep her voice level and steady for the whole thing, which for me made it especially beautiful, because for once talking poetry in public just sounded so entirely proper—like that was the only way these things should be talked of, you know? And seeing those two—seeing Shaz, with her hair all piled up on top, and with that beautiful dark-coffee skin of hers framed all in silver down her back, and with Alex holding both of her hands—well you know it was quite something for me to be finally seeing these two ladies of ours standing side by side up there and making everything official. Even if they had already been together for eleven years.

I reckon I wasn't the only one with a lump in my throat at that point, is what I'm saying.

Anyway, we got through all of that bit pretty much OK, and then through all of the official bit of them going out next door and signing things—and there was a fair bit of sniffing and blinking at that point too, actually, and even a little shower of applause when they came back into the function room hand-in-hand—but then, once Xardine had got us all piled onto the number fifty-five bus, and we were all heading back up to The Downs for the party—well by then, forget about lumps in throats; everybody was pretty much in the mood to cut loose and party. Shaz truly looked like she was *shining* with relief—silver earrings swinging, head thrown back—and she had pieces of confetti threaded all the way through her up-do, I remember, despite all the big signs that there'd been on the pavement outside the Town Hall forbidding that particular piece of bad behaviour. Alex had gone a bit quiet, I noticed, and was sitting a few seats back, next to her best mates Zed and Peggy. The rest of us were filling the whole of the top deck and laughing and carrying on all of the way up Mare Street—and I was laughing too, but when I noticed Alex going quiet like that, I couldn't help but be thinking about the words of that Shakespeare poem again, and the sheer bloody overall strangeness of what I'd just sat through. Two grown women, standing up there and making vows to each other—because I tell you, when I was a child, at the Secondary School over on Chapel Street, it would have been six strokes across the hand to have been even caught imagining such a thing. And now here I was, fresh out of a British Town Hall, watching everybody coming all over tears and cheers of approval, and joining in with cheers myself.

Like all of those things I'd had installed into my head back then could be melted away with one stroke of a Lady Registrar's pen.

Like that O'Riordan boy had never written out all the names he called me in bruises.

Like that vindictive devil Father O'Halloran had never even existed.

The bus ploughed round its corners, and then, there was the girls' tower-block—all eighteen ugly storeys of it—and there was that ridiculous sign at the edge of the grass, the one saying *Welcome to The Hackney Downs*—like that made sense of anything at all.

§

I want to go back for a minute to those two strangers up on the living-room wall.

A week before—so, at the end of March, last year—Shaz and Alex had summoned Xardine and me over for a planning dinner, to go through the arrangements one final time. The usual incumbent was still in pride of place over the gas fire at that point, which was Frida Kahlo, in a big framed poster—all scarlet jungle-flowers, behind a big black suit—but this little antique wedding-photograph of Alex's that I'm talking about now was already propped up on the mantel-piece underneath it.

My first thought was to wonder what on earth it was doing there, because it looked so out of keeping with the rest of their stuff. I mean it wasn't just black-and-white, but positively Victorian-looking. However, my second thought, when I looked a bit closer, was that this had to be a family photo of some kind, because your man there in the picture and Alex herself were the absolute spit. I mean, the two of them had not just exactly the same jawline and hair—and haircut, actually—they also had exactly the same way of staring back at you from inside a jacket and trousers. You know? Wary, but sure as hell taking no nonsense. So I asked who the man was, standing there on those white marble steps, with his bride on his arm—I asked Shaz, actually, because Alex was out in the kitchen at that point doing the coffees—and she smiled a bit oddly, and said I should get Alex to tell that particular story.

The man worked as an asphalter, Alex told us, when she came back in with the tray—and his wife was a laundrywoman, and the white marble steps they were standing on belonged to St Peter's church over in Clerkenwell—like I should have known that—and in fact, I was right about him being family, because this man in the picture was actually Alex's great, great grandfather.

Which explained the hair and jawline, I guess.

It also made sense I reckon of why Alex had got the picture out there in the living-room. Both of her parents were dead and gone now, and she only had a couple of elderly aunts and maybe some distant cousins still living back in Italy; about Shaz's next of kin I only knew that they were all still alive alright, and still all based around Reading, because that was where they'd first landed in the seventies. However, none of us had ever met them. Not even her parents. And so I guessed that maybe what had happened was that the girls had been talking about family—about the invitation list for the Town Hall, probably, or at least to start with—and that maybe Alex had got this old photograph out of a box or whatever to help with that conversation, and then just left it accidentally out there on the mantelpiece before it got put away again.

Knowing that this funny-looking couple were directly related to our Alex certainly made you look at their wedding-picture a bit differently. It made their faces jump a lot closer to you, you know? It made you think, for instance, about whether the bride had to make her own wedding-dress, and also where on earth she might have gone to borrow those tight-looking satin shoes. Whether he'd borrowed his suit for the day. And the thing I supposed you noticed most of all was the woman's flowers. White carnations, she'd got—and I mean not a bouquet, but a whole great water-fall, maybe thirty or forty actual blooms at least, plus a display of ferns and white ribbons that reached down to her feet. I asked Alex how on earth they could have afforded flowers like that if your man there was out on the roads and his wife was taking in linen, and Alex said well they would have had no family with them on the day, on account of their having been the very first people from their particular town in Italy to come over, and so maybe by filling his wife's arms with flowers like that, and then having their photograph taken, well maybe that would have been his way of telling everyone back home that they'd landed on their feet. Maybe he even sent copies of the photo back to the old country—Alex said—because we're like that, us Italians. You decide to do something, you put on a proper show, even for the family who aren't there. Even if you can't afford it. Aren't you Irish the same?

I'd never really heard Alex making any big deal about being Italian before, and she seemed almost angry about it all of a sudden—and to make the atmosphere even odder, I noticed

Shaz just then going back out into the kitchen quite abruptly. This was apparently to just get some more milk, but also I think it was because she didn't want anyone looking at her face for a minute—and that made me wonder how she was doing with *her* whole family thing. I knew from Xardine that they definitely weren't coming, but also that just ten days ago Shaz had phoned her mother to try and talk. The way Xardine told it, somebody in Reading had literally taken the phone out of the woman's hand and slammed it down.

Shaz always claimed she was fine with all that, and that she'd reconciled herself to all of their nonsense years ago. Her ma and pa were first generation, she always said, so what else could you expect? But still—can you imagine?

Once Shaz had come back in, and Xardine had asked her if she was all OK, and Shaz had replied that yes of course she was, Alex carried on with telling us her story. Galleatti, she told us the couple's name was, and that the link was on her mother's side. And never mind the flowers, she said, look at the bride's shoes. Even women's *shoes* had buttons, in those days.

I can't remember now if it was me or Alex who first had the idea of including her family in my speech. When I think about it, maybe it *was* her idea.

§

We talked all about the catering, that evening; we talked in detail about which particular tracks each of them wanted Dom the DJ to play at the party afterwards—about how many cans we'd need to get in—but at no point at all in the evening do I remember us talking about Shaz's flowers. And so yes, I did think that the white cardboard box from the florist over in Dalston was a trifle on the large size as I was fetching it up to the flat at eight o'clock that morning—especially when I discovered that it almost wouldn't go in the lift—but no; it never occurred to me to take a look inside. So it wasn't until the three of us were standing around the dining table and watching Shaz carefully lift back the folds of tissue paper that I realised what Alex had actually done.

Shaz gasped, when she saw them. Because there they all were—three whole dozen of the things, and all in that kind of weird, sugar-icing white that only carnations ever truly have, so that they looked almost not real until you started to smell them. And all lying on a great raft of ferns and white ribbon they were, so just exactly like in the photo. And when Shaz carried them off to look at herself in the bathroom mirror, they even trailed all the way down to her hem, just like they had for Signora Galleatti. That florist had certainly done a great job—and Alex had really made her point.

When Shaz saw in the mirror how beautiful the flowers were, and what a vision they were turning her into, she had to look away quite sharply, and ask Xardine for a tissue to save her face— and it's funny, looking back, that none of us saw those tears of hers coming. After all, there'd been so much in the papers and on the telly that spring, with people arguing about whether these ceremonies of ours were going to be 'real' or not—about whether they were going to be as real as an 'actual' wedding—all that sort of bullshit—that I reckon we should have known. We should have known that whatever we'd told ourselves in the run-up, a day like this was going to present us all with some fairly tricky moments in the mirror.

This time, it was Alex who left the room, I noticed. And obviously this was just one small hiccup, but I can't say it did anything much to settle my nerves.

§

About an hour into the party, I was looking at that photograph again—and holding on tight to my second whisky. The party was going great, but I was still having some fairly serious trouble with getting my head round how I actually felt about it all.

In particular, the Powers and I were having trouble with all the memories that were still winging their way back into my head from Blackrock. One of them—which was nowhere near as sharply focussed as that picture, but the Powers and I were working on that—was about another man called Jacky, who'd been my mother's second brother. There wasn't much to remember about him visually—I mean, not his face or anything, because this Uncle Jacky was dead before I was born, and if there were any pictures, I was never shown them. But I did know that people said he'd gone over the water as well. He'd been on the roads, people said, tarmacking—so just like our handsome Mr Galleatti, then—and had died young of it, in some godforsaken room or other in Kentish Town. And this first London Jacky had never got married either.

Anyway, the picture wasn't giving me too many clues, no matter how hard I stared—and next thing I know, Shaz is squeezing my elbow and suggesting now might be a good time for my speech. So what could I do? Ready or not, I got my notes out of my pocket again—for just about the twentieth-*first* time that day, I reckon—and waved across the room for Dom to get the music turned down. He was just getting going with some Dusty Springfield, I remember, *What Have I Done to Deserve This?*—which ought to have made me laugh, but it didn't—and while he was fading her down I took a last fortifying sip of my drink, gave myself a bit of a shake, and then started proceedings off by doing the whole traditional Best Man thing. You know—up on a chair, and tapping my glass with a knife from the table. Ms. Springfield piped down gracefully, Xardine gave a couple of calls for quiet—and that was when I made my first big mistake.

As I say, I was standing up on a chair at this point, and this chair was right in front of the girls' living-room window. Next to the table. And the table was all still covered with the food, and so without thinking about it—because why would I—once I'd got everybody's attention, I turned around and went to put my almost-empty whiskey-glass down on the window-sill instead. So that I'd then have both hands free for my notes, you see. However, bending down to park my glass on the sill meant that I could also see down through the window, and for a whole eighteen stories. The dead-looking patch of grass down at the bottom there started coming up towards me—way too fast for comfort—and the glass of the window itself seemed suddenly very thin. I swayed like a fool, and even had to grab at somebody's shoulder.

Embarrassing.

Anyway, I got myself together—checked my notes—and then, before I got launched into the speech proper, I checked around the room to see whereabouts the happy couple themselves were standing. Because they were the whole point, right? I hesitated, and looked again, and discovered that I'd been right the first time; Shaz was there alright, but Alex wasn't with her. I checked again—and there were some shouts of *speech, speech* from the back of the crowd at this point—coming from Zed, I think—and so after a bit more of all this Shaz rolled her eyes, like she always does, and said she'd just pop out into the hall to see where herself had got to. Maybe she's in the bathroom checking her tie again, she said, winking at me.

Next thing I know, Shaz is standing back in the doorway, looking shocked, and indicating over her shoulder that something's gone wrong out in the hallway. I indicate to Dom to put Ms. Springfield back on for a bit—I crack the old joke about the best-laid plans—and tell everyone to grab themselves a fresh drink. I'm sure she's fine, I say to Shaz as I pass her in the doorway, because it's probably just some after-party stress. Butches, I say, what are they like?

§

She looked like someone had just slammed her up against the wall.

And I mean it; Alex looked exactly like she'd just been socked. So I went a bit closer—she was right down at the end of the hallway, right down by the back of their black-painted front door—and now I could see that she had both her eyes screwed up tight and was contorting all of the muscles of her jaw. Grinding her teeth, I think. And I knew how much was churning away inside of my own head, by this point—what with the drink, and the Town Hall, and dead Uncle Jacky—and so I was pretty sure there must have been a fair bit going on inside Alex's head as well. That chewing jaw of hers made me think of the dreadful old ride they always used to have at the Dublin City Fair each year—you know, that awful wooden spinning thing that pinned you to the boards and then dropped the floor away from under your feet. Christ, I thought, your woman here is clearly in some kind of trouble.

Alex ordinarily looks like she's slightly sun-tanned—well actually she looks like a woman with Italian great-grandparents, I suppose—but right now she was as white-faced as your proverbial ghost. I touched her arm—gently—and said very quietly who it was, and then I asked her how she was doing. Hello Jackyboy, she says, though clenched teeth. Turns out I'm not quite ready for this, she says; I thought that I was—she says—but really, after all, I'm not. At that point, I found myself putting my hand on her jacket sleeve again, and her muscles were like she'd been carved out of wood. I don't know why, but that surprised me. I would never normally be as close to a woman who was this upset, I suppose, and certainly not to Alex, because closeness was never her style.

That's Ok, I said to her, there's no rush. You just take a moment to get yourself together—I said—because after all, speeches can always wait.

She was grinding her teeth again, and whatever force it was that was keeping her up against that wall, I could see it was really ripping right through her. So I tried again. But you've done it, I said; the hardest part's over. Come on, I said—but Alex shook her head and snorted a kind of horse-breath down through her nose. Zed and Peggy came round the corner from the living-room at this point, to see if they could help, but I put my hand up to let them know it was OK, but that we just needed to give Alex a moment to get herself together. I said: Come on my friend, Shaz is waiting. And I've written this speech for you two specially, you know, just like you asked me to. No gay men's jokes, I promise, and no Blarney either.

She still wasn't moving—it was as if Alex thought leaving the wall would somehow mean she'd drop through the floor for real—and so I tried again. If it helps, I said—touching her arm—do you think maybe your great, great Grand-Daddy in your photo there might have felt just the same? When he got his own lady back home, after making all those fancy promises?

I've no real idea what I meant by that, but I knew I had to get Alex moving somehow, and the sentence arrived, so I used it.

After what felt like a very long moment, she breathed; then

she leaned forward from the wall, and let me hold her by the elbow while she got her legs back under control. Then she shook off my hand, opened her eyes, and walked unsteadily up the hall.

As we got back into the living room, Dom cut the music completely, and because of that, everybody looked round; Zed and Peggy helped me to get her over to Shaz, and Shaz kissed her quickly and took her by the arm. Alex flicked a hand through the quiff of her hair, at that point, and tried a kind of smile. It didn't really work, but at least she looked a little less white-faced than she'd looked out there by the door. Then she turned to me, and said—very quietly—well what about this speech of yours then Jacky. Let's be having you.

Well, you know what they say; stay calm—and don't look down.

§

And as you can imagine—I said—holding on tight to my bit of paper, and trying hard to keep the shakes out of my voice—I've been thinking about making this speech quite a bit. In fact, I've been thinking about it ever since Alex and Shaz first asked me to do them the honour. And the thing is—I said—like most things in life, it turns out that the hardest part is just getting yourself started. I mean—I said, looking around the room—take the traditional opener on these occasions. 'Ladies and Gentlemen'; well, given the present company, that hardly covers all of our options, does it?

There was quite a good response to that. Over at the back, I could see Salty and Mz Michelle, laughing out loud under those little matching cocktail hats that they'd worn—and even Zed, who let's face it in that suit and tie was practically passing—well even Zed was cracking a grin. It's always good to get your first laugh, and so I pressed on.

However—I said, splitting my words up carefully, and doing that whole inverted-commas thing with my fingers in order to really make the point—'Ladies' and 'Gentlemen' will probably have to do. However—I said—I'm sure that none of you gathered here today need me to tell you that this is not in many ways an especially traditional occasion at all. In fact, I'd rather describe it as a very special one. And, as some of you may have noticed, we have got two very special extra guests here with us to help us celebrate that fact—here I indicated the photo, on the wall—to help us celebrate, that is, the glorious fact of our dear friends Alex and Shaz becoming legal at last. Now, I know several of you who've been all the way up here to the eighteenth floor before have been wondering where the lovely Ms Kahlo is today, and who the two newcomers who have dared to take her place up over the gas fire here might be. Well—

At this point, I realised from all the craning necks that not everybody could really see. So I asked Todd, who was standing across the table from me, next to his partner Roger—Todd and Roger were just about the longest-running couple there, I reckon—I asked Todd if he wouldn't mind hooking the picture down and passing it up to me on my chair.

Which he did.

So now I was actually holding the photograph in my hands, as well as my piece of paper with my notes.

Which also wasn't easy.

Thank you for telling me all about these two, Alex—I said, going back to my notes—and I do hope I'm going to get all the details right for you here. As it happens—I said, holding the picture right up, so that everyone could see them—the two people in this photograph were newly hitched themselves, when this picture was taken, and they also happen to be family. These two beauties are called Signor and Signora Giovanni and Angiolina Galleatti, and I am happy to tell you that they are Alex's great, great GrandDaddy and GrandMa. So now you all know where Alex gets that handsome Italian jawline from—I said— and that got a laugh again, from Peggy as well as Zed this time, and so I showed the photograph round a bit more, making sure everybody could see more or less what I was talking about, and then cracked on some more.

Angiolina and Giovanni are standing on the steps of St Peter's Church—I said—down over in Clerkenwell there—and here I tried pointing in what I hoped was more or less in the right direction, insofar as I could manage that without actually dropping anything—and that's where the two of them had just gone and got themselves married when this picture was taken. Alex has looked all of this up, you'll be pleased to hear, and according to the London census forms for the relevant year it looks as though the two of them had only been living in the capital for less than twelve months at that point. And after the wedding, the story doesn't end there, because they then went on to have two children, both boys, the oldest of whom—and I made quick check of my notes again just here, because I really didn't want to mess up this particular detail—yes, that's right, the oldest of whom, also a Giovanni, was Alex's, mother's, grandfather.

I thought about taking another sip of my Powers at this point, because I knew from my notes that I was now on the home stretch. But then I remembered where I'd put my glass, and decided that I didn't want any repetition of that moment with the patch of dead grass flying up suddenly to meet me halfway.

Alex wanted these two lovelies to be with us today—I said, taking a deep breath instead—Alex wanted them to be here so that they could enjoy the party. Well, I hope they are enjoying it. And also—and I know that this idea is a bit of a long shot—I said—given that this is now the twenty-first century, and these two got hitched in 1886... but what I'm trying to say here, Ladies and Gentlemen—and all denominations in between—is that I really hope that if Angiolina and Giovani *are* up there somewhere, and if they are looking down and watching us all celebrating today, well, I really hope that they approve of what they're seeing. As bold pioneers themselves, I hope that they approve of the new world they are helping to bear witness to here in this room, and I really hope that they realise—

I was getting quite seriously croaky at this point, as you can probably imagine. But, I stuck with it. After all, I'd written it—

and now I meant to say it, lump in my throat or no, rising-up grass or whatever. And so I took a moment, and then just went for my big finish. I really hope that they approve of seeing all of us gathered here together today—I said—because we too, yes, we also are our dear friends' Family. And as their family, no matter what today's ceremony is called in law, we wish them—

And then I had to stop. My voice was starting to shake just about as hard as my piece of paper, and Mary Mother of God I was angry. Like why was I even having to say all of this shite? Why wasn't one of the men from Shaz's family up on this chair and doing the right thing by her on this amazing day—and why, when it came to this moment, was I actually not thinking just now about the girls and their story at all, but about those awful grey trees at Blackrock Station on the day I left home. About my Uncle Jacky, found dead in his room in Kentish Town, and about that damnable young bastard named Fiach O'Riordan. About how I still hate even the word *confession*. And why was it that I was suddenly imagining—as I stood there, with the lump in my throat getting harder—that all of the words I had inked down on my bit of paper there might just as well take flight, and wing themselves out through that cold window next to me, and head all the way back over the water to Blackrock—all the way out over those London trees and streets and houses and right back to the place that I once called home—only to crash themselves then against all the closed-up doors and windows of that town, breaking their necks like so many lost and exhausted birds. Because I knew, you see, that for me there was absolutely no-one who wanted to hear those words, back there; that there was no-one left back there who could have any idea at all as to why watching these two darling women become a married pair in all but fecking name was making me actually physically have to stop myself from crying out loud up there on my chair. And me a grown man of thirty-four. With insurance, and work, and everything...

It was Miss Salty who saved me—and trust a queen to do the right thing in a crisis, eh? I'm standing there, like an open-mouthed fool, with everyone wondering where the hell my punchline is, when suddenly she lets forth with her very best opera house *Bravo*. And I mean we're talking your actual Royal Opera House here, because our Miss Salty's voice is quite the banshee's when she puts her mind to it. And that fair broke the tension, I can tell you; in fact, it absolutely smashed it. Whatever wave of feeling it was that had been gathering itself in that room, it just bent itself in half and then crashed right over us. It was cheers and tears, all round. And then, right on cue, Dom slammed the music back on, and—of course—it was Ms Joplin herself this time, delivering the lyrics of Alex's vow at absolutely top and neighbour-offending volume. I mean, Janis was singing like she really meant to break down some walls. People started kissing and dancing all over—and Alex herself grabbed Shaz by the waist and really went for her. I mean, she really took her woman's face off, right there in the middle of the living-room.

Right in front of everybody.

Leaving me... well, leaving me standing up there on my chair, feeling the cold air coming in off the glass again, and also something inside of myself, something which I didn't want to put a name to, but which I knew was called rage, even though it felt like ice.

§

After that, I drank—and everybody else danced. Dom really went for it, with his music; we had Lorraine Ellison giving us *Stay with Me Baby*, we had *Young Hearts Run Free*—we even had CeCe Penniston giving us *Finally*, which I hadn't heard in years, and which got even Roger and Todd throwing some shapes. Later, I can remember Roman and Vee getting it together during one of the slow numbers; Roman's hands were working their way steadily downwards, and as Peggy pointed out to me as she and I stood on the edges and watched them, it certainly looked like those two were going to be next ones taking the trip down Mare Street to the Hackney Town Hall.

The girls' living-room was chaos, by the end. Glasses everywhere, crisps walked into the carpet—and a destroyed-looking cake-platter standing all by itself in the middle of the living-room table, rimmed with the remains of some great cream and meringue creation which somebody must have brought, but which nobody really wanted to eat. About half past ten or so,

Dom faded away his last track, and then Xardine and I did our best to start persuading people to leave. We offered to help stay and clear up, afterwards, but you could tell that the girls really wanted some privacy now. Also, Alex had definitely had one drink too many, which was something I hadn't ever seen her really do before. I got my coat, and used the toilet, and then the very last thing that I did in the flat that night was to go back into the living room. I'd seen that somebody—maybe it was Alex, but I don't know for sure—had put the Galleatti's back up on their nail, and before I set out for my bed, I wanted to look them in the eye for just the one last time. I wanted to know if those raw-looking expressions they both had were anything to do with what Alex had said to me out there in the hall. *Not ready for what*, I asked them, breathing all over their glass—but they kept very still, and said nothing.

Ah; the dead, I thought. *All the living, and the dead...*

In the bathroom, I'd noticed that the carnations had disappeared from where they'd been laid back down in the bathtub, and that there was a trail of water all over the floor. I wondered who Shaz had given them to, to take home. Salty, probably—or maybe Vee and Roman, to wish them some of that traditional tossed-bouquet good luck.

Yes, I was jealous.

§

It was freezing, outside, and I don't suppose I was walking too well as I finally set off for home. When I got to the edge of the Downs, I turned myself around to look back up at the girls' tower: I wanted to see if I could work out which of the remaining rectangles of light belonged to their living-room. I tried counting upwards—twice—but got lost both times.

I turned left, and then right, and then cut down left to Mare Street. It wasn't the most direct route to my bus stop, but I'd decided I wanted to take another look at the Town Hall. Just to make sure that this whole crazy day had actually happened, I think. But somebody had been out with a broom already, and the confetti was completely gone. In the end, I just carried on walking; it may have been freezing, but I really needed to take some time before I reached my bed.

I needed to ask myself how it was that I still remembered that O'Riordan boy's first name.

I needed to ask myself how it was that Father O'Halloran had once made me believe in hellfire so completely; how it was, I mean, that he'd so exactly convinced me that it was never going to be a young man called Jacky up there at his altar rail on a wedding-day.

That it was never going to be a man called Jacky having his face taken off in front of everybody, and absolutely loving it.

Because until I was up on that chair, you see, I had never quite realised that I still absolutely believed all of that stuff. At the grand old age of thirty-four.

§

And now—I don't.

Now, I know what Alex meant as she leant against that wall—and as it turns out, being ready for your big day has nothing at all to do with history, or the law. It has to do with the fact that the one thing you can never be ready for is love.

For instance; six months ago, a handsome stranger smiled rather oddly at me while I was busy minding my own business on the southbound Bank Line platform at Camden Town. And as I was coming back to my flat here this morning—which is the self-same top-floor flat to which I dragged the aforementioned stranger, that same night, and where we now share a double bed—this morning, in order to get my keys out of my pocket, I had to put my two bags of shopping down on the front steps.

I put them down carefully—because the steps are stone, you see, it being an old house, and I'd the bottle of champagne for tonight—and I was just fishing for my keys, when my eye was caught by the little slip of paper under our doorbell. You know, that little slip of paper with your name on it, the one that you write out and then slide into the little brass frame, after you've moved in, for the benefit of your postie? And of course these days that slip of paper has two names on it; it has mine—because I've been resident here halfway up the Camden Road for nearly four years—and now, as of twelve weeks ago, it has Jonah's name as well. Added underneath with a pen. And when I saw that label, that's when I felt it; I felt this great wave of absolute fecking *certainty* come up off the step and up through my legs and stomach and straight into my chest and heart.

That's right; *certainty*. The certainty of being able to turn a key and then walk up our stairs to a waiting man just flooded right through me. Like a drink—or rather, like the blade of some beautiful hot sword, running me through right there and then, and making me actually stagger on our stone front doorstep. How could you ever be ready for a feeling like that?

Well; I suppose none of us ever realises how much weight we've been carrying until it's lifted.

And so yes, this is what I now know, one calendar year after that strangest of days; that what you can't ever be ready for, ladies and gentlemen—of all denominations—is Happiness. And personally, I don't think we should even be calling it by that name any more—at least, not until I've had the chance to get used to it. No; I think we should try calling it vertigo. You know—that sensation you get, when the floor disappears? Or when a lift rises too fast, or falls; the sensation that catches you sometimes in dreams, when you think that the glass in some high window is about to give way, and you can just imagine how your arms are going to flail and your hands turn to claws in the air...

Well in fact, you're going to discover that you're flying.

Only do it if you're holding the right person's hand—that

would be my advice. That, and do ask *not* to have the 10 a.m. slot, when you're making your booking down at the Town Hall together.

203 Camden Road

I'm not sure if time always *does* go forwards.

For instance, you'd think I'd be used to being married by now—but I'm so completely not. When I see the little slip of paper with Mr and Mrs L. Lennard written on it, under our bell, I still wonder who that is. And when I hear Len whistling and making a mess in the bathroom in the morning, I still really can't quite believe that it's him that's going to come out through the half-glass door and let me catch him walking around in just his vest and pajama-bottoms while I do his egg. And then, when on a Sunday morning he stubs his cigarette out and says, Right then Mrs Lennard, let's get you back into that bed of ours, well he still makes me feel like it's our first time.

Oh god—that stupid cold hotel room on our honeymoon. With the gas fire that ate all our shillings, and then still wouldn't work. Honestly, I couldn't stop shivering.

I don't mean it's bad between Len and me, because it's not, it's wonderful. In fact, it's better than anybody ever told me. But— every time—every time we do it, I mean—I go back. Sometimes it's even like I'm back right at the very beginning, staring at my dress spread out on the bed on the actual morning of our wedding, with those stupid big duchess-satin sleeves that I'd chosen, and me still not believing it was finally going to happen. With Mummy tapping on the door and asking, Are you alright in there darling, and me wondering whose arms and legs are these anyway?

When does it stop feeling like that, I wonder?

Last night, after we'd finished, Len was stroking my belly. He was saying, Where's my little fish then? I know you're in there little fish, because your mum says you are—and then all of a sudden he looks up at me with those great big eyes of his, and he says in his kidding posh-voice, Well you do realise Mrs Lennard that when this child of yours goes to the big school, the year is going to be nineteen seventy-something. Imagine that, he says, stroking me again. Nineteen seventy-one, nineteen seventy-two, nineteen seventy-three—and I had to close my eyes when he got to that one, because I can't imagine that far ahead at all.

Before you get pregnant, you see, the future's just an idea; then, when you do, it turns all very solid and slippery at the same time.

It's like there's this number, on a door somewhere, and you know what the number on the door is—because that's your actual due date, you see—and also what street it's on—because that's your month—and also you can picture the door itself quite exactly, even the colour, and handle, and everything—but you still can't for the life of you imagine what everything's going to be like on the other side. Inside the actual room.

When I asked my nurse about it—about the specific day and month, I mean—she said, Well Mrs Lennard I can't calculate your exact due date for you unless you can tell me the exact date of conception, and as you know that's not really possible, because of all the different ways that different women's bodies work. And I said, Oh but it absolutely is possible Nurse, because I can tell you exactly. I'm absolutely sure it was the same afternoon as we moved into our new flat, you see—which I *am* sure of, because I remember very distinctly Len and I were both in so much of a hurry that afternoon that we didn't bother with our usual precautions. Right there on Mr Christoforides awful mattress it was, just as soon as all our cases were up the stairs. I mean even before I'd got any sheets or pillowcases on the bed or anything. And so I told her what date that was—the date of when we'd moved in here on the Camden Road—and she flipped through some pages in her little desk calendar and then smiled and said, Alright Mrs Lennard—alright Maureen, she actually said—since it'll make you happy, I'm going to say you're due at lunchtime on Thursday the ninth of May; Thursday the ninth of May, 1966. Then, of course, to be professional she said again, But you know it never does quite work out like that, don't you Maureen—but it was too late, you see, she'd said it out loud, and so from now on May the ninth is absolutely as far as my brain can see. When I finish this cup of tea, for instance, my head will be thinking to itself oh never mind people saying to each other on the bus *Good Lord only three weeks now till Christmas*; as far as I'm concerned, the only date that matters is one hundred and fifty-nine days away.

Mostly, everybody is telling me that everything's going to be all brand new and lovely once I get myself through that door. You know; new flat, new baby, new life—but I have to say that most mornings it doesn't feel like a very lovely prospect at all. I don't mind being sick, but I do mind being scared, and some mornings I feel like it might be April at least already, and the door's right there in front of me and way too big and dark for comfort.

So you see what I mean about time sometimes jumping all over the place and whatever.

§

Actually, this flat's dreadful. I mean look at it. *Maisonette,* that was what I was imagining before Len and I got married—everything all very Ideal Home. White paintwork and everything. Instead of which, here we are; two rooms plus lav and kitchen. And right up at the top of the stairs. Sloping ceilings, a bomb-site out the back, and this bed is shocking.

But we've talked about it, and I'm sure Len's right when he says that it makes sense for us to stop here until after the baby comes. Saving up for a proper place will take longer now of course, what with me having stopped work to look after myself, but with the rent at forty-five shillings a week it shouldn't take us for ever. The wallpaper's a challenge—you do have to sit with your knees up to have a bath—and Mariette down on the ground floor told me yesterday she's got her mice back in again, which sounds awful. But not everything's bad. There's a David Grieg's just round the corner for basics, and the buses from across the other side of the road all go straight down to Camden Town itself if I need anything extra. It's cold, because we're right up under the roof, but there's no actual damp as such.

Roll on Christmas then.

§

This year, he gave me my favourite perfume, Elizabeth Arden's 'Blue Grass'. And he asked me to put it on before we went to bed. Smashing.

§

Len says nothing's an accident. He says our bodies must have just wanted the baby, and I can't say I mind—well not most days I don't, in for a penny, etc—but I still haven't quite worked out what I'm supposed to do with all the actual time. Christmas itself was fine, because we went up to Walthamstow to Len's mum, who's lovely, but now that that's all over and done with I find I don't always know what the days are for. Afternoons, especially. I'm knitting a bit—or trying to, and failing, which is dreadful of me when you think of how many pattern-covers I must've done for work at the Studio. Yesterday, I even tried getting dressed and putting my face back on, as if I was going back in. It ate up some time, but then I felt like a right fool sitting there all dressed up and nowhere to go, so now I'm back in this dressing gown again. I've read all my leaflets from the Health Centre for the ump-teenth time; I've cut out and tacked some new curtains for the back window—oh and I've been pacing. Not that there's a great deal of pacing you can do in two rooms plus lav and kitchen, I must say.

Mummy did warn me; most ladies get a bit energetic in the fifth month, she said.

Mind you, she also said I'd stop feeling sick around now, and that's not happening at all. Putting my feet down first thing still makes me feel like the lino's on a boat.

The thing I miss most about the Studio, is all the other girls. I miss having somebody to have a laugh with. Len makes me laugh of course—but it's not the same.

My feet are really swelling up something awful today.

§

Happy New Year. A hundred and twenty-nine days to go. We stayed in bed till lunch-time.

§

I asked Mariette about the bomb-site, and she says she actually remembers that one. She and her mother lived here all the way through, she says, but she recalls that one in particular because it blew out all their windows—there was glass all over her mother's front-room carpet, apparently. Now of course it's all just a jumble of bricks and sycamores out at the back there, almost like an actual wood, really, but with bricks instead of soil, and also that awful corrugated-iron stuff nailed up all the way around it to stop the kids getting in. Horrible black branches they are, on the trees, like some sort of dreadful skinny arms and hands. Grabbing at things, when it's windy.

She's a treat, Mariette—always with that same thick orange powder on her face and eyebrows pencilled half way up to the hairline. I suppose when she was my age that was the fashion, and she just got stuck.

Honestly, I think they should demolish all these old houses. Get the Councils building something proper for all the young people like Len and me.

§

Len's mum says love will see us through. 'The early years', she calls this bit—but she doesn't have to look at those awful sooty tree-branches every bloody morning.

Pardon me.

I must finish hemming these curtains.

§

One Hundred!!!! And, as well as that, this afternoon, something actually happened.

Len and I have this game we play where we take it in turns to list all of the things that we're going to have one day in what

151

Mummy calls 'Later On In Life'. Top of Len's list is always his blessed Ford Consul—Teal Blue, he says it's got to be—and top of my list is always a fridge. Anyway, this afternoon—Wednesday—I was getting the milk-bottle in off the kitchen window-sill, which is all the fridge we've got in this place, hence me mentioning our game—and just when I was doing it, I happened to look down out of the window, and there he was. A man, coming right up our front path. Middle-aged, lightly thinning on top, but very sort of clean-cut and definite in his movements, if you know what I mean. Very smart. He was wearing a car-coat, three quarter-length, and very nicely tailored. In some sort of a light-weight tweed, I should say from the way it was hanging, plus what looked like a very good pair of brown shoes. So: casual dress. Meaning he can't be working in the City or at a bank or anything—and the thing was, he was also carrying a parcel. A sort of thin, square brown-paper package it was, possibly a present—and so I reckoned that what with the package and also those brown shoes this was probably him dressed up for a visit. Also, just as he came up the path, he did that thing that men always do when they want to look their best. You know; a quick flick over the hair and then a quick twitch at the tie-knot.

I couldn't think who this parcel he was carrying could be for—because no disrespect, but he didn't look like the sort of man to know the Walker family—and so I was just wondering which of the four bells he would be pushing, when I felt the door go downstairs.

I should explain. It's a great big black old thing, our downstairs front door here, and the point is that it doesn't stick exactly, but it is very tight-fitting. Even when it hasn't been raining. Which means, you see, that the air on the stairs here is sort of permanently sealed up, and so you always know when somebody's opened the main door downstairs because our front door up at the top here in number four always makes a funny sort of a noise in sympathy. A sort of *whump* noise, is how I'd describe it. And the thing is—bear with me—there hadn't been enough time for this man in the smart coat to have rung number two or three, and for them to have come down to let him in—and not even Mariette, on the ground floor—and so whoever he is, he has to be somebody who's got his own key. D'you see?

And then, only just about five minutes later, I heard the music. Coming right up through our living-room floor it was. Right through the new rug. I couldn't make out what it was at first, but then there was definitely the sound of a trumpet. All on its own, it was—I mean I expect there was a band playing along with it as well, but I couldn't hear that, not through the rug and floorboards and everything. So it sounded like the trumpet was just floating—or actually, I'd say it sounded more like the trumpet was just thinking out loud to itself, rather than doing anything like what you'd call a proper tune—and coming up through the floor like that it sounded all rather far away and like it was feeling sorry for itself. I didn't mind, though. Rather suited my mood.

I don't know what sort of music you'd call that really. But then I never really did pay attention to the radio at work; I just left all that sort of chatter to the other girls and concentrated on whatever I'd got to finish drawing before five o'clock.

Anyway, this business with the music coming on almost immediately after this man had come up the path got me thinking. We're up on the top floor here, like I said, which is flat number four, and Mariette downstairs is number one; there isn't any basement, so that leaves just flats number two and three by way of a possible explanation. Flat number two is the Walkers, at the back of the first landing; they're a Jamaican family, with three little girls who are lovely, and Mr Walker who works on the buses, and his wife Mrs Walker who looks after the little ones. Well, as I say, no offence but I couldn't quite see the man in the smart coat bringing the Walker girls a present, or having a copy of their key—and anyway, more to the point, the Walkers are right under Len and me's bedroom, and this trumpet was definitely coming up through the floor in the front room. Which leaves only flat number three. The bedsit.

Mr Pierce; that's the name on the bell.

And would you believe, I've never actually met him? Despite the fact that he moved in just a fortnight before we did, apparently—and this is nothing to do with me avoiding anybody, I hasten to add, but according to Mariette (who knows everything) this Mr Pierce in number three does keep rather odd hours. This, she says, is on account of him working in what she calls 'the business'. Which means basically a nightclub or something in the West End, I think—and Mariette always puts the phrase between inverted commas like that because that's the sort of work she used to do herself when she was younger, and she wants you to think that she's still all a bit glamorous and mysterious-looking, despite those dreadful long housecoats she's always wearing.

Anyway, the important bit here is that Mariette says this mysterious downstairs neighbour of ours is young. A nice *young* man, she always says—and that man in the car-coat didn't look young at all. Closer to forty than thirty, I'd say. So that doesn't really add up. When I first looked out of the window, I even thought for a second that it might be our landlord, Mr Christoforides, but I've seen him several times, and he's nowhere near that smartly dressed, so it's all a bit of a mystery.

Possibly, of course, Mariette's just got it wrong—she did say she'd only seen Mr Pierce once or twice to actually speak to.

While I was getting Len's tea, my mind kept going back to the visitor's way of walking. If I was sketching him as a figure at work—for an advertising lay-out, say, or a fashion illustration— capturing his walk would be what I'd go for first. He gave you this sort of leaning-forward impression—you know? A bit *sprightly*, if that's not too funny a word to use. And he was wearing sunglasses—did I mention that? All of which was rather striking-looking on our front path, if I'm honest. What with the bricks of the path itself being all half black, and all those filthy privet-bushes getting so big and overgrown down the side.

So if the gentleman who likes trumpets *is* Mr. Pierce, well he's rather a smart and well-dressed sort of a person to be living in a dump like number two hundred and three, I must say.

It lasted a good half hour, the music, and then I didn't feel the front door being opened again until just before five.

Oh stop it. Now you really do sound like Len's mum. She's for ever talking about the neighbours.

§

I can't say this has been the best of days. I had hoped the feeling sick was over. However, at least I've had plenty of time to think, and finally I think I've got it all worked out about the Wednesday mystery.

Here's what I've come up with.

For starters, I reckon the man in the car-coat *was* Mr Pierce— and I know Mariette says he's young, but I reckon her powers of observation aren't what they used to be. And the music—well the music must have been in the parcel. D'you see? Square, thin— stands to reason it could have been an LP. And I reckon Mr Pierce had just bought it down in town, and then not been able to wait to hear what it sounded like, and so he'd popped back here in the middle of the afternoon, put it on for a quick listen—loud enough for me to hear, though I'm sure that wasn't deliberate— and then got himself changed and gone back down into town around five o'clock for work.

It more or less makes sense, I think—although it's a shame I'm not still going in to the Studio, because then I'd be able to describe the music to Shirley who works on the next desk, and she'd be able to tell me its name. She's always up on the latest thing, is Shirley.

So; mystery solved. If I had the energy, I suppose I'd be jealous of him, Mr Pierce, but as it is I rather like the idea of people still being able to go shopping on Oxford Street even if I can't.

Funny how you don't really know what other peoples' lives are like, even right under your floor.

I'd better get Len's tea.

§

Wednesday. Seventy-nine.

I wasn't in the kitchen, so I couldn't check out the window, but as soon as I felt the door go I did look up at the clock—and it was three o'clock again exactly. Ironing's my least favourite job of the week, even at the best of times, and when that trumpet started coming up through the floor again it actually cheered me up quite a bit. Rather kept me going. It was a bit louder, today, and when the long slow bit arrived just before the end it seemed to just go round and around for ages. And today, when it got to that one very long high note, well I swear I felt such a flutter. She really caught me. Kicked me, actually, and I'd say that was definitely the most I've felt our little fish move so far. I put my hand on my stomach, and the trumpet came round again for that finishing bit, and I swear she must have been able to hear that bit as well because she kicked me right on cue. Hard. I had to go to the bathroom.

I finished the ironing, and then at about ten past five, I felt the door go downstairs again. I happened to be in the kitchen at this point, because it was time to think about cooking, and so this time I did look out and check the path. Mr Pierce was wearing a different coat today, a three-quarter-length sheepskin which looked brand new and rather expensive—and his walk was different as well. I couldn't say how, exactly, but as he left he definitely walked over to the bus stop as if he was in a hurry about something. And there must have been no bus in sight anywhere up the Camden Road at all, because all of a sudden he stuck his arm out and this taxi pulled over. He climbed in, and they headed off down towards Camden Town. Possibly he was late for work, and I suppose in his line of work you really can't be. The show must go on and all that.

I made myself some more tea, but I didn't drink it—and the next thing I knew the door was *whumping* to tell me Len was coming up and I hadn't got the table laid or anything.

He didn't say anything though, just got on and helped me.

I'd been down to Camden myself as it happened, earlier, and bought us kippers from that cheap place opposite Palmer's. On the bus home, I thought the smell coming up from my bag was something awful, but tonight when I unwrapped them from the paper I was starving all of sudden, and I thought they smelt— well I thought they smelt like me. And d'you know what? I didn't mind. So everything's strange at the moment, and that's that.

Why is it always three o'clock when the music comes through the floor? And why on a Wednesday again?

§

This morning, I couldn't face the bus at all, so I decided I'd just walk round to Greigs. I knocked on Mariette's door to ask her if she needed anything, and while we were talking I mentioned that Len and I still haven't actually met our downstairs neighbour. Mariette said, Well I'm not surprised, because I think young Mr Pierce keeps himself to pretty much to himself in the daytimes. Because she'd said that, I asked her again what sort of age she thought he was, and she said she thought probably twenty-one tops. And you can tell he's in 'the business', she said again—like she does, and lifting one of her eyebrows so high this time I thought it might get actually stuck. Oh really, I said, what makes you say that? Oh well, she said, you know, just a certain way of moving us people involved in the profession often have. And, of course, you never hear him in the mornings, do you, she added, as if that explained everything. I was going to ask her if she ever heard any music coming down through her ceiling on Wednesday afternoons, but I couldn't think of a way of doing that without seeming nosey. Then she mentioned about wanting some more peroxide, and so I waited while she went and found her handbag and then I trotted off round the corner. Or hauled myself, rather, because honestly I feel like I've got a bag of potatoes or something strapped to the front of me these days.

Anyway, I've thought about it some more—about the music, and everything—and now I think I really *have* got it all worked out properly at last. I've decided that Mr Pierce and the man in the brown suit must be two different people, and that the explanation of all this only-on-a-Wednesday routine of theirs is that the two of them must be what Shirley at work would call 'friends'. You know. And the older one—the one with the dark glasses—I think he's probably working in sales, somewhere fashionable, and I think he must visit us only once a week because he has some sort of a regular weekday business appointment for which he gets time off. And with regards to the music, well I think he gave that long-player with the trumpet solo to young Mr Pierce downstairs as a present for his birthday.

No, I take that last bit back—I mean who knows when Mr Pierce's birthday is. But I reckon the rest of my story makes sense. It certainly makes sense for instance of Mariette saying young Mr Pierce looks as though he works in the West End, because Shirley at work, she knows someone who works in the box office at the Duke of York's theatre, and she says he's absolutely that way inclined, and so are a lot of other people in that part of the world.

Of course, it surprised me, when I first got this idea. I mean the idea of there actually being a pair of them, and in the flat right underneath us. And my first thought, if I'm honest, was that maybe I ought to feel upset or shocked or something, and that I ought perhaps to mention it to Len in case he wanted to say anything. But then my second thought—well my second thought was that actually I wasn't shocked at all. Not even upset, really. And I've sat here for a bit longer, and I think I've got that bit of the story worked out as well.

Once, back at our house, it was the first time Len had ever come over for his Sunday lunch. And I was very nervous, mostly about Mummy meeting him of course, on account of him being only an electrician from Walthamstow as she puts it, and I was standing up in my bedroom, waiting at the window—and the point is, I remember Len coming up our front path with exactly the same spring in his step as Mr Pierce's friend had that first Wednesday. You know, with that sort of 'I know where I'm going' look about him?

And I think that's why I'm not shocked, you see. I mean, I know it's not the same thing—I know it's not like these two downstairs are an actual courting couple or anything, not like Len and I were by the time we'd got to the stage of Mummy inviting him round on a Sunday like that, because that would be a ridiculous thing to say—and besides, this friend of Mr Pierce's must be a good thirty-eight if he's a day, so it's hardly love's young dream down there in number three, is it—but still, feelings are feelings. Aren't they?

If you think about it.

Mind you, you do read such dreadful things about them some-times, don't you? About their being arrested, and all that sort of thing. In the Evening Standard.

Oh what do I know about anything? Too much time on my

hands, that's my problem. And Mummy did warn me; she said, You do know darling that the baby will make you think odd things occasionally. I said like what, and she said, Oh you know, out of character things. You'll see.

§

Len's coming home for his dinner in the middle of the day today, because he's working on a job just over in Kentish Town. Keeping an eye on his best girl, he calls it. And I do look a sight, I know that, but when he comes home today I don't want my husband to sit down and eat his dinner, what I want is for him to take his coat off and touch me. Straightaway. That's right. Right in the middle of the afternoon, and right on this table. There I've said it. Mummy never mentioned those sorts of feelings, did she?

§

It's been getting much colder again. Nothing like last year, thank God, but I've still got my green coat back on over my dressing gown. We had the trumpet under the floor again today, but I put the radio on and just kept ironing. Seventy days.

There was a girl at school, I remember, who used to talk a lot about what she called the sex side of things. Dora, Doreen—I don't remember. Anyway, she used to cheat at games, and acted like she knew all about it. Sex. But she can't have done, can she? I know I didn't. The first time I came on, for instance, I had no idea at all—and Mummy wasn't much help, telling me that the most important thing was to always make sure the bathroom door's locked. You really mustn't make a fuss when you're attending to yourself down there, she said, because they really don't like it. She meant men, of course. I was always most careful to make sure your father didn't have to see anything untoward in his own house, she said, while he was still with us. Then she had her little cry, as she always calls it.

Len has really helped me with all that. Helped me to stop hearing Mummy's voice in my head, I mean. Not quite so often, anyway.

Actually, I think Daddy would have liked Len, if he'd lived. A lot. Daddy would certainly never have said half way through that first Sunday lunch, Oh really, and where is Walthamstow exactly?

§

Well, I finally met him! I finally met the mysterious Mr Pierce. We were just about to pass on the bottom stairs—me going down slowly, him coming up two at a time—but then just at the last minute he said, Oops, unlucky, and so we stopped, and then just stood there for a bit and talked. Mariette is quite right; he *is* young. Dark corduroy trousers, black roll-neck sweater, quite long fair hair. A bit like that Georgie Fame, but thinner and with a much softer voice.

I started things off. Hello, I'm Maureen from upstairs, I said.

And he smiled and said, Oh hello, I'm Leonard from number three but do call me Lenny. Which must have made my face go funny or something, because he said, What? and I said, Well that's my husband's name. Lenny. Leonard. Mr Lenny Lennard, I said, Would you believe it! Oh yes, he said, I sometimes hear him go out in the mornings. Oh I'm sorry, I said—because I suppose he meant his front door in number three does the same thing of making a funny noise as ours, which must be very annoying if you're trying to sleep late. Then he asked me, What does your husband do, and I said, He's an electrician, and he said, Oh really, and to be polite I asked him what he did for a living himself, and he told me he's a dancer, which means Mariette was right. What kind of dancing is it that do you do then, I said, and he said, Oh you know, musical things mostly. I was doing The Talk of the Town for a stretch at the end of last year, do you and your husband ever go to the Hippodrome? Well yes, I said, once or twice we have been there, I do like to go out in the evenings or used to anyway before this happened! Meaning my tummy. And he laughed. Well then, he said, you might even have seen me working away in the background. Then he said he was hopeful of another job soon, because he'd just been to a dance-call—whatever that is—and we both wished each other luck and good morning.

I'd been nervous about meeting him—I mean, I knew we were bound to bump into each other eventually, but still—and I don't know whether it was just the accident of his name being the same as Len's, but when it came down to it, I actually liked him straight away. He has a lovely smile, which you don't always see on a stranger do you? I wanted to say your friend who comes to visit you Wednesdays, what does he do for a living, but of course I couldn't possibly. More pregnancy nonsense on my part I suppose, or perhaps I was just trying to be polite.

It was very nice to put a face to the name, anyway, and actually I called that up to him just as he was reaching his landing. He shouted down, Likewise! And we both laughed. Well, two Lens in the same building—it is funny when you think about it.

I really do believe that's the first time in my life I've ever actually known I was talking to one. Really. There was that Mr Hobdell, of course, who used to call monthly to deliver our fabric samples at the Studio, but he was a very unpleasant person. Especially that one time. Putting his hands all over Len's arm like that, just because Len had come to pick me up wearing a short-sleeved summer shirt. Saying, Oh I had no idea being an electrician was such a manual profession, Mr Lennard. Whatever that meant.

No I don't think Mr Hobdell counts, and anyway I'm sure that behaviour was more to do with him being a drinker than anything else, because he was always absolutely reeking of it no matter what the time of day. I wonder what happened to him?

§

So there was a little drama here in flat four at the end of last week. Another little scare from yours truly. I woke up in the dark feeling cramps again, nothing too unusual to start with, but then they turned into really bad ones. I wanted to leave it till the morning, but Len said no chance. He had to run round the corner to the telephone box—and then get me down the stairs of course. The roads were icy again, and it seemed to take for ever in the ambulance. Black ice, the driver said, when Len shouted why he was going so slowly. But it turned out to be nothing after all, in the end. They have said I need to rest more though.

Mariette's been popping up to see me, which is nice, and Mrs Walker brought me up a ginger-cake—home-made—and her three girls to visit as well.

There was music from downstairs again today. I didn't go to the window, but then later, at about six o'clock, I did, because that was when Len had said he'd be in from work, and I just fancied catching him coming up the path for a change. I wanted to see how he was walking.

I know. How silly.

§

Well Len and I have had our first big fight. He said he would get the tea tonight to save my back, but then he made such a fuss about it that honestly it would have been less trouble if I'd got up and done it all myself. I told him to just do some potatoes and a tin of peas, to go with—it was fish-fingers—but then he kept on shouting things from the kitchen like how the hell were you supposed to get it all ready at the same time and where was the bloody tin-opener anyway. The fish-fingers were actually black, when he finally brought them through. I said I'd do us some dripping toast instead, and that was when he shouted at me. And I shouted back. Can you believe it? I hadn't got dressed, you see, but then what with him cooking for me like that, I felt like I ought to have done, and so now I was feeling cross and ugly as well as useless. I'd never heard myself shout at anyone before, never mind using language. Changes, changes, changes. What would Mummy say indeed.

§

Awful. Really awful. Look, my hands are still shaking, because it wasn't music coming up through the floor this time, oh no, it was shouting. Straightaway. And so loud, you could hear the actual words. Go on then, why don't you leave me—personal things, that nobody should hear. Plus lots of language. And it wasn't as if I could slip my shoes on and go out and let them get on with it, because I was having a really bad day. The shouting went on for a bit, and then it went quiet, and then suddenly the next thing you know there is this sort of strangled-sounding screaming noise, I mean something really not quite human in a way, like something had got itself caught in a trap or something. Really. And then there was a bit more shouting, then a great crash of something going over—and suddenly I thought *but what if something awful happens*—like in the papers—I mean you do read about these things and I have no idea what I was thinking of, not really, but anyway I grabbed my housecoat and went out onto the landing to have a look. I suppose I thought I might be going to go down and knock on the door and say would you mind at least keeping the language down please. But then it all happened so fast. I was about four steps down, when the other man—not Leonard, you understand, but the other one—this other man came bursting out of their door looking like thunder, and then Leonard came out onto the landing after him. And Leonard was in just a pair of underpants, if you can believe that. Anyway, he grabbed the other man's arm, like he clearly wanted to stop him going, and then they started actually fighting each other right in front of me, grabbing and slapping at each other like I wasn't even there. One side of Leonard's face was in a dreadful mess already, I suppose because the other man had hit him with something, inside, so I started shouting would you just stop it now please, and then the door of number two opened and out came Mrs Walker to see what all the noise was about. Giardina, her youngest, was right behind her, trying to hide in her mother's skirt, and I've no idea where the other two were, inside I suppose because there was crying. I shouted out, It's alright Mrs Walker, you just take Giardina back inside, because I could see that the little one was absolutely terrified, but I think Mrs Walker was so surprised by what she was seeing that she just sort of stood there. And quite right too, in a way, because Leonard—Mr Pierce, I mean—Mr Pierce was practically naked as I say, and also there must have been alcohol somewhere, because you could smell that too. There was blood coming down all over his face, from where he'd been hit, and some of it was even getting onto his underwear. So I shouted again—first of all, Stop it—to the two of them—and then, Go inside again, to Mrs Walker. She looked down at them rolling about on the floor—made a funny sort of sucking noise with her lips—and then she scooped Giardina up and took her back inside, and my goodness was she making a point of slamming the door when she did that, and you could hear the bolts all going bang, bang, bang down the inside. I shouted, again—well actually I was almost screaming myself by this point, I reckon, and holding onto the bannister—and that sort of interrupted things. The two of them stopped grabbing and punching at each other for just a moment, and then Leonard got up, and then the other one as well, and after that all three of us just sort of stood there for a bit looking stupid. The older man wasn't looking up at me at all at this point, because obviously I didn't really matter, and there was this terrible noise all the time of them panting, and the smell of drink, and also the blood that was running down Mr Pierce's face and then everywhere. All of it, honestly. Absolutely awful. He—the other one—was looking absolute daggers at Mr Pierce still, and I don't know why, but I suddenly felt in my mind that Leonard or Mr Pierce was the one I had to look after in this situation, and that I had to make this other man go away. And so, Are you alright, I said—as loudly as I could—Are you alright, Mr Pierce? Are you alright, Leonard?

As soon as I said that—as soon as I called Mr Pierce Leonard—the other man turned his head. Like a dog would, you know, just before it goes for you? And suddenly I realised what an absolute fool I was to have even come out onto the stairs at all, on account of there now being absolutely no-one else there to look after me if things got worse. I pulled my housecoat round over me, to protect the baby, but also to make him see how big I'm getting, because I was thinking well he probably won't dare have a go if he sees me sideways. I was standing a few steps up above him on the stairs, and I think that probably helped. Anyway, he stared at me, still panting, and somehow the look on his face was made very much worse by how smart and expensive his shirt and tie still were despite the fighting and his collar being torn. That all looked so very wrong, you know? He bit his lip—and was about to say something I think, but then very quickly Leonard, I mean Mr Pierce, interrupted and said, Yes thank you Maureen, I'm fine—and speaking very properly, he was, but also with his voice shaking just like mine had been. Which was not surprising really, because his face was looking like something out of a butcher's window. Yes, thank you Maureen, he said, a bit softer now, the two of us are just fine. So his friend knew then that we were acquainted, you see—because I had said Leonard, and then Mr Pierce had answered right back and called me Maureen. I mean he at least knew now that I wasn't just some random interfering stranger, but rather that Mr Pierce and I were friends, or at least acquaintances. And that seemed to knock him back a bit, I must say. He stepped back a pace, and ran his hand over his face like he wanted to clean himself up a bit—like he wanted to make himself presentable or something. Alright, he said eventually; if you say so Len. And then he looked across at young Mr Pierce again, and I could see suddenly that he—the older one—was trying very hard not to cry. I couldn't think what it was at first, he looked so peculiar, but that was definitely it. All twisted sideways and jumping about, his face was. Just like Daddy's used to, at the end.

When I got back upstairs, I tried to calm myself down. I made myself a pot of tea, and then I sat down here at this table. And then of course it started. The music. Except that it was so loud, this time, that you could hear the band and the drums and everything. I didn't understand what was happening, at first—because I mean how could they be sitting down and listening to their LP together, when the two of them had been knocking all sorts of business out of each other just a moment ago?

But then I heard the noises.

The men's noises.

And that's when I realised—I mean that's when I realised why the two of them always play that same record on Wednesday afternoons, and why it's always so loud. D'you see?

It's so I won't be able to hear them.

And now—well now, they obviously didn't care. I mean the music wasn't covering up anything at all. It was coming up through the floor just as loud as you like—but they were being even louder. Both of them. And I don't know why, but of all the things that I could have done for myself while I was sitting here at our dining table and hearing that extraordinary racket coming up through my living-room floor, I started laughing. And I mean actual, proper, laughing-your-head-off laughing. And I had my hands on my tummy at the same time, you see, because as well as hearing it I could also feel all of that drum and trumpet business carrying on right inside me. As if the band were doing their big number right there inside of me.

Really roaring, I was, like I absolutely didn't care either. Like Mrs Lennard from flat number four absolutely didn't care *what* sort of a noise she was heard making.

I've no idea how long I've been sitting here now, but I really mustn't get cold. Len will be home soon, and we'll have our tea, then we'll wash up and it'll soon be time for bed.

Shock. Yes, that's what this is. I'll just go and get my coat.

All quiet downstairs.

§

And what if it hadn't been me who'd heard them, eh? I'm not saying Mrs Walker would, or Mariette, but somebody else might've been perfectly capable of calling the police. Or going to Mr Christoforides. And then where would they be? Out on the street and probably in the papers as well.

§

A bunch of violets—just outside our door. There wasn't any note or anything, but who else could they have been from? When Len saw them on the kitchen window-sill later I told him I'd bought them for myself, and he said, Oi that's my job, and kissed me—and thinking about all that noise there'd been yesterday, I thought, how funny; when the baby comes, the boot's going to be on the other foot. I mean, if I can hear two grown men coming up through our floor, they're certainly going to be able to hear a new-born baby coming down through their ceiling. But then I suppose the noise a baby makes is the sort of noise nobody ever gives two hoots about. No matter what time it happens in the afternoon.

No, I don't know why that should be the case, but there it is. That's life, as Len's mum would say. Not Mummy; she'd say shall we perhaps talk about something nice now darling, if you don't mind?

§

I tried to get down the stairs and go round to Greig's yesterday—please don't ask me why. Mummy was supposed to be coming to visit me at about eleven o'clock, and so I absolutely should have stayed in bed and just waited for her. But for some reason I decided that I had to get Len and me a Fray Bentos steak and kidney pie for our tea tonight—and the whole thing turned out horribly. I had to sit down on somebody's front wall and pant like I don't know what. Which is where Mummy found me. And, of course, she totally got on her high horse again, all about number four being most unsuitable for a woman in my condition and why on earth had Len got me living in this dreadful part of town anyway. She even got around to saying whatever would Daddy have thought if he was still with us, but I held my tongue. I mean imagine if I'd told her about life in number three—she had enough trouble getting over meeting Mrs Walker and Giardina out on the landing. I thought she was actually going to choke, she was so surprised when she saw that beautiful little girl and her mother for the first time.

Actually, I was quite tempted to tell her about Mr Pierce and his friend regardless, just to see the look on her face.

Anyway, the upshot of all this drama is that Len says we have to move before the stairs become completely impossible for me. Obviously, I'm in no fit state to go round looking in newsagents windows, so we've agreed that we'll just have to look in the Evening Standard like everybody else does. I've sorted him out some change for the phone calls already.

Speaking of the Standard, there was a story last night about two men being arrested up at Holloway. Three bus stops away, in other words. A record producer, they said, and somebody else. I tore the page out, and deliberately used it to wrap tonight's peelings. I mean they even included the men's actual addresses. I ask you. I hope they're proud of themselves in their newspaper office, whoever it was decided that was a necessary detail.

§

Looking in the paper has been all rather disheartening. Len likes the sound of one place we spotted yesterday, called Hamlet Gardens, ground floor, but it's right over in Hammersmith. Well Ravenscourt Park, which I think is Hammersmith more or less. Also Len said the landlord didn't sound too friendly on the phone and was going on straight away about not taking coloureds or Irish, so if I'm honest I'm hoping Len'll come back home after seeing it tonight and say he doesn't think it's right after all. In case he does, I've marked out some other places in today's first edition. I hauled my dressing gown on this morning, knocked on number three and asked Mr Pierce would he mind picking up a Standard for me down at Camden Tube as soon they arrived, because the sooner you get looking the better, it seems—and he was very nice about it I must say. I hadn't seen him since that afternoon, but neither of us mentioned it, and I didn't mention the flowers either. He said he was sorry to hear that Len and I are moving out, and then he told me that he's got a new job coming up at last. Some big new American thing he said, at Drury Lane, and that I really ought to come and see it later. His face looks all healed up now thank goodness, which is just as well I suppose, as I imagine that bruising could be rather a problem in his line of work.

There were quite a few options in today's paper, and I've put rings round them all. Two are quite near here—one's just down on Royal College Street, actually, so barely a bus stop away—and then there are three more possible-looking places further afield. One in Clapham, one in Balham with a shared bathroom, and then one right over in Ladbroke Grove. Although people do say the houses over there are terrible, so on second thoughts, I'm crossing that one out. Honestly, I can't help thinking sometimes that you might just as well stick a pin in the paper and choose that way—I mean you never really know what a place is going to feel like until you actually shut the front door behind you, do you? Clapham I suppose might be good, in a way, because then Len and I could take trips from Clapham Junction. Show baby the sea next summer. But on the other hand, that Park bit of the Ravenscourt Park address might mean I'd have some proper trees outside my bedroom window for a change.

Oh where's my box of bloody pins.

§

I know I shouldn't have, because my back is going to kill me for it later, but this morning—can you believe it—I actually got on a bus. Mariette put the most dreadful scarf on over her hair to come with me, in a sort of hot-pink-with-lime-green chiffon, and people didn't half stare, but it was good to have her arm nonetheless. And the conductor was smashing. When the bus came, the step was too high, but he pulled, while she pushed— and gosh he was strong. Looked like he could have been Mr Walker's cousin. It was the number twenty-nine, and so we were able to get that all the way down to the big HMV on Oxford Street—the flagship store, I think they call it, and I'm happy to say that the young man behind the counter there was ever so helpful. I told him all about the trumpet coming up through the floor—well not *all* about it, obviously—and he said, Oh that definitely sounds like Mr Davis. Like I ought to have known who that was. Anyway 'No More Blues' this new record that I've bought the two of them is called, and apparently it's just come out. I didn't wrap it, I've just kept it in the bag from the shop, and when Len and I leave first thing tomorrow, I'm going to slip that to Mariette and ask her to just prop it quietly up outside their door later. Mr Pierce didn't put any note with his violets, I know that, but I've decided that I am going to leave one with my present, just saying it's been lovely being your neighbours and so on. You know—I hope the new show goes well for you, and also that everything goes alright in the future for you and your friend. Because I do think it's important to say thank you to people who have helped you to get a bit braver in your life, even if they don't actually know themselves how they've done that for you.

Last night, with Len—my Len—I was on top, which is all we can really do now, in bed—and when I was getting close I started hearing that trumpet under the floor again. I mean not for real, but down inside me. And goodness that made me let go. I tried to hold on, but I just couldn't, and then once I'd started it just went on and on and on. Bloody hell, Len said afterwards, you mare, you absolute steaming mare. You're the best girl a bloke ever had Mrs Lennard, he said, d'you know that? And I was on top of him still when he said that, and also he'd put his hand on my belly, like he does sometimes afterwards, and so you see he was right inside me and also feeling where the baby is all at the same time. And then he looked right up at me—right into my heart—you know—and I'd been kissing him so hard at the end there that I think I might've hurt my mouth a bit, and I was worried it might be going to actually split in two if I smiled too much, so I had to keep my face straight, but I was actually thinking; we're alright, us two. We're really alright, and maybe Hamlet Gardens won't be so bad after all. And there's the front door now—*whump*—

8 Hamlet Gardens

Wednesday evening, rather late.

Today was a busy day, and long.

On the radio, first thing, the grating voice of Home Secretary May, talking once again about her policy of making people 'unwelcome'. Not the best of starts, it must be said. I prayed, here at the kitchen table, and asked once again for strength. Leo had a client somewhere right up in the wilds of Wembley this morning—Stonebridge Park, I think he said—and so set out well before me. Another family needing to take their landlord to court over overdue repairs. After that, he was due all the way down near Lambeth North, where one half of a gay couple has asked for help on behalf of some non-English-speaking neighbours. So no rest for the wicked. Once he'd gone, I washed the breakfast things—noticed through the window that the leaves are coming out on the trees of the park, over our back-garden wall—then sat down here to start my emails. All the time, that word of May's was running through my head. Does she have *any* idea what it means?

Leo texted me from Hammersmith to say that the Piccadilly line was down again, and so come half past ten I had to use the car to get out to Heathrow (it being Wednesday, and my turn to take the midweek service at the airport chapel). The traffic was fine, but I did have to do a nifty left-right-left to get around that new set of road-works that's appeared on King St.

When I finally got to St George's, there was somebody already sitting just inside the door. That's not too unusual; people often use the chapel as a place to sit and be quiet before they go through Departures. However, something about this particular traveller caught my attention. He looked much the same age as me, late forties at least, and—this struck me quite forcibly—he was holding his hands clasped in front of him in exactly the same way as I do. His head was only half-bowed, and what I could see of his face gave the impression of someone almost entirely locked away inside their own thoughts. He looked quite deeply troubled, if I'm honest. Perhaps frightened. I was careful not to disturb him, and went quietly into the vestry to change. By the time I re-emerged, however, his place in that last pew on the left there was empty. I was sorry, but not surprised; we often have people visiting St George's who haven't otherwise entered a church or faith-room in years, and the last thing they want is to be confronted by a working priest.

Leo says people may be terrified of flying, but they're even more afraid of being caught praying.

My *doppelganger*'s departure meant that I then read twelve o'clock prayers to no-one. However, all was not lost. As the morning weather lifted, the light coming in through our one piece of stained glass turned momentarily rich and strange; I spoke the necessary words, and the silence received them.

After the service, I was due to spend this afternoon at the parish office, but that was not to be. When I checked my phone, I found a text asking me if I could drive immediately round to Harmondsworth. To the Detention Centre.

That initial message was short, but quite clear; the detainee in need of a volunteer witness at his preliminary interview was a young male, aged twenty-six, and originally from Lagos. So far, so good; however, as soon as I got there and checked my phone again, I discovered that things were in fact more complicated. The young man's visa was deemed to be essentially in order, but initial checks by the Home Office had revealed that there was a significantly disputed criminal record back in the country of origin. Meaning that there was bound to be aggressive questioning over his relationship with his proposed UK hosts. Then—and this really didn't make things any easier—I discovered that two extended family members had driven all the way from Birmingham, hoping to visit him in custody. They'd come from Edgbaston, they told me, and the journey had taken them over three hours. Nonetheless, my first job was to explain to them that there was absolutely no chance of them getting inside. They'd brought two young children with them, imagining I suppose that this was going to be more or less like visiting somebody in hospital; the kid's presence meant that when I arrived in reception, the duty officer was already firmly digging in his heels. His arms were crossed, and he was insisting—via the microphone—that they be removed from the building before he'd even answer any questions. I know he will have had his instructions, but both the mother and her youngest child—a toddler—were already in tears. In her case, of anger. The family didn't know who I was, of course, or what I had to do with anything, so it wasn't easy to get them back outside; however, after some negotiation, I managed.

I explained that because I was only there as an observer, their relative and I wouldn't be allowed to really communicate, but assured them that I'd bring any significant news back out to their car later.

So that wasn't much of a good start either.

Once I'd been ID'd and buzzed through, everything was more routine. The corridors looked as unfriendly as ever, and the windows just as high. There was the usual chemical smell— and I have to say, that although this must have been my seventh or possibly eighth visit to the Centre, I still find the physical details shocking. In the interview room itself, most of the detainees simply keep their eyes locked down onto the metal of that sharp-cornered desk-top. Or up at the face of the clock, which is the only other fixture. Younger men tend to give their answers through clenched teeth, I always notice, I suppose to avoid losing their tempers completely.

I also noticed beads of sweat, today, on the side of this particular young man's neck.

Checking through all of the preliminary paperwork again took the best part of an hour, and then—and only then, after the teeth of several fine combs had been ostentatiously broken over two incorrectly logged dates of travel—did the H.O. representative see fit to push a further folder across the table and say he'd noticed that the proposed hosts (Edgbaston) had made the mistake of saying—in writing—that they can only provide two weeks less than the stipulated minimum period of accommodation. Which might well of course invalidate any right to remain.

The young man himself hardly spoke at all.

When I got back out into the car-park, the family had gone. And I know this is shameful, but I have to say I was glad. Glad, that I didn't have to listen to any more children crying, or women shouting.

Harold Cyril Andoh, this young man was called. And he was extraordinarily beautiful, and dignified despite everything. I want to record both of those facts.

Coming home, there were planes stacked above me all the way along the M4, and the road traffic was just as bad. Trying to get my mind out of that interview room, I turned on the car radio— only to be confronted by May again, still pronouncing the word 'people' as if she'd rather be holding it with tongs. I switched her off, and slipped in a CD, the one of the Scottish Chamber Orchestra playing Bach that Leo gave me last Christmas. I tried really hard to make the music send me somewhere else—really willed it to replace or re-order my thoughts—but the trick didn't work. I was stuck with that smell, on my clothes, and the image of a pulsing vein on the side of Harold's neck. You wouldn't think that the *air* inside a room could be made hostile, would you, but it can.

I just wanted to get home and shower.

When the front door closed behind me, I started crying—in my own hallway—and that was partly out of relief, I think, but also because I must have been holding my breath ever since the car-park. When Leo finally got home from work, he had to give me another one of his lectures about not letting my volunteering get to me. Christ, what would I do without that man's love to sustain and correct me on a daily basis?

Before dinner, I had to make two long and rather difficult phone calls, both to names on my care home rota. Mrs Keidan is going downhill fast; she seemed hardly to know who I was this evening, much less why I was calling.

I must talk to her daughter. Tomorrow.

We did the washing-up together, and then Leo had case-notes to write up, and I finally got back to my emails.

We didn't watch the news.

So as I say; a long day—but before it ends, there's something else that I want to try to get down here. Leo says if I'm going to keep a journal, then I have a duty to record the positive, not to dwell only on the darkness of the world, and he's right.

Here it is:

As I was leaving St George's, I noticed that somebody had pinned a postcard to our prayer-board. That's unusual; ordinarily, people just leave folded-over scraps of paper, with their messages hidden away inside. I knew immediately what the card was—a Caravaggio, his 'Madonna of Lareto' from Rome—and even though I was in a hurry, seeing it quite stopped me in my tracks. Perhaps it was having just read that text, the one from the Centre.

Because—after all—she's a traveller too, this lady. A migrant. If I remember correctly, the legend of the painting says that the house whose doorway she's standing in has just been airlifted out of Palestine by a night-time air-crew of angels—rescued, from some invading army. Croatia, I think the angels took it to first, then across the water to the Adriatic coast—and what an image that is; an entire house, spinning slowly down towards you out of some seaside dawn, in a flurry of rainbow-feathered wings. And today, as I was looking at her—at her face, and at the heavy and about-to-cry toddler that she's got balanced on her hip—I noticed something about the painting that had never registered before. The doorway of her house has dirty brick walls framing it, and a high doorstep, and a heavy, black-painted door-frame—but no actual front door. All that surrounds this woman is a peculiarly gentle-looking rectangle of reddish-brown darkness, and it is from this darkness that she seems to have just emerged, as if answering some unspoken appeal.

In other words, there is nothing to keep you out. There is nothing that could be slammed in your face; nothing that could be used to exclude, or deny, or humiliate. And I had such a sudden sense of home, looking into that darkness. Of a place of safety, and of refuge.

What a word *that* is, Mrs May.

On reflection, I think it must have been the man with hands like mine who pinned up that card. Indeed, when I was watch-

ing him—when I was watching his hands, and trying to read the expression on his face—I think he must have had it all ready and written in his coat pocket. And after he'd left, of course, I could have taken it down; I could have un-pinned it, turned it over, and read whatever explanation or petition he'd inked on the back. But I didn't. Of course I didn't, because I was in a hurry; I was trying to find my car-keys, and already wondering how long it was going to take me to get through the Heathrow one-way system and find that easy-to-miss right-hand turn-off for Harmondsworth—but now—now, when it's late, and quiet, and I have time to think about that empty door-frame, I realise that I had no need at all to turn that reproduction of Caravaggio's picture over in order for me to receive its message. We are all travellers. We none of us know our final destination, or whether we'll always be safe. And if we forget that about each other, even for one day, then our hearts will harden, and cease to do their allotted jobs.

That's as clearly as I can put it, I think.

Before I close this and go to join Leo in our bed, I ask that my unknown visitor of this morning may land safe and sound, whatever dark waters of fear and doubt he is now flying miles above: I pray that all the broken families may one day be re-united, and all loves equally honoured.

I pray that everyone may know the meaning of that always-open door.

Amen.

I think I might undress out here in the kitchen. Leo's bound to be asleep—he said that visit down by Lambeth North station was a real bugger.

40 Marine Parade

Todd and I were never expecting this place to be our final destination. We'd been Londoners all our adult lives—five different boroughs, we reckoned we'd lived in between us—and three of them together—Ealing to start with, then Hackney, and then finally Lambeth, in that lovely house next door to the Choudry family. So ending up down here was never meant to be the plan. But then, when we found this flat, and saw the light flooding into it straight off the sea—and then, when the estate agent reminded us that the town was only an hour and twenty-four minutes from Victoria—we straight away knew two things; that I'd be able to keep on working until retirement, and that we'd be happy here. I can still remember how, on that very first mad afternoon when we found this place, Todd spent several long minutes just looking out through the living-room window. And then he smiled, and turned to me, and said quietly, Darling, this is going to be it.

As it turned out, we only shared our beautiful view for seven years; seven, out of our total of thirty-six. And then, one cold Wednesday afternoon in March, Todd just wasn't there any more. He wasn't on the stairs; he wasn't in the kitchen, and he wasn't in the bed.

For the first few weeks, I thought the silence was actually going to kill me. I used to hear it straining at its leash as I stared out of the kitchen window, first thing; I used to hear it trotting behind me as I carried my mug of cooling coffee from room, to room, to room. Kitchen; hallway; living-room. Living-room; hallway; kitchen. Sometimes, the silence would thin, or hide, to try and trick me into thinking it had fallen asleep—but it never offered to move out. One morning, there was a patch of early sunshine on the kitchen wall, and for some reason the colour reminded me of a tin of yellow paint that Todd had once used to do up an old chair in our second place, in Hackney. The thought of him dancing around with his headphones on and his trousers all splashed in exactly that sort of intense sunlight colour made a noise come out of my throat that sounded almost like laughter— and the silence loved that. It swallowed it whole, then whined for more. I tried going upstairs, but that didn't work at all; our bathroom here is right up under the roof, and the combination of a sloping ceiling and all the tiling round the bath seemed to amplify everything. I even tried running all the taps at once, to create a distraction, but that didn't seem to work much either. Next, I wrapped my fist in one of our best white hand-towels, then started punching out the mirror from the front of the bath-room cabinet. I didn't actually get the glass out of the frame, but I certainly smashed it, and for a couple of minutes there was quite a definite respite, as if the silence was rather shocked, or at least pretending to be—but then it just gave itself one of its hairy, shaggy-dog shakes, and tried something new. One minute

I could hear it chuckling to itself, hyaena-like, and the next it had turned itself into something more or less completely human-sounding. First, there was a medical voice, quite reasonable, and sounding pretty much like the young doctor we'd started off with last November; he was explaining to me how any fool could have predicted our outcome just as soon as Todd found that first lump, so who on earth did I think I was trying to kid by the time we'd got to the last week of February? Then, the voice got bigger, and scarier, and whoever or whatever it really belonged to started to drown the doctor out with something much worse. Finally, the bathroom started to fill up with what sounded more or less like an orchestra, except that this one was made up only of strings. Or vultures.

I was sick. The dark droplets that came up out of my stomach unfurled in the toilet-bowl just like those miniature Japanese paper flowers, the ones that he always used to get me at Christmas-time—and yes, I know it sounds mad, but that was really what those first few weeks on my own were like. I started drinking whiskey, in the mornings, and was really only aware of time passing when I noticed that the sun seemed to be getting stronger on the windows. It never occurred to me to turn down the heating, and eventually the flat started to get too hot to even breathe in.

At the crematorium itself, you see, I'd just worn a suit, despite how freezing it had been that morning—because there was no-one to remind me to take an overcoat, I suppose—and then, when I'd got home afterwards, all I'd wanted to do that Wednesday was put on the thickest woollen sweater I could find. And after that, I'd simply never found a reason to take the sweater off. I was even sleeping in it, in fact. And so when one morning in the second week of May I heard all the radiators coming on, and then happened to lift one of the sleeves of this sweater to wipe my face, it smelt absolutely revolting. I tried to pull it off, but it put up quite a bit of resistance; eventually, I carried it downstairs into the kitchen (our flat here on the seafront is on two floors, did I say that?) cut up the wool with our kitchen scissors, then stuffed the whole thing down in the bin. Then, I went back upstairs, splashed my face, looked at the bedroom clock—and walked straight round to the other side of the bedroom. After taking a deep breath, I opened up my side of our wardrobe. One thing seemed to lead to another—I remember tearing at some dry-cleaner's plastic, with my hands—and then the next thing I know is that I'm walking to the station, fast, and wearing a suit and tie.

As if catching the seven-o-nine still made sense.

I think what I should try and write down next is what happened on Christchurch Road, and how I found the empty house.

§

Before, my feet always used to get me to the station without me even thinking about it. They'd turn right out onto the seafront, right up Montague Place, left at the second corner, right again and so on. No attention required. But that morning, they stopped.

Because of a noise.

I looked left, across the road—Christchurch Road, so only ten minutes away from my train at most—and I could see immediately that the house the noise had come from was a ruin. I mean, it was filthy; dirty yellow bricks, dusty windows, cracked black paint on the nineteen-thirties-looking front door—and brambles, almost entirely obliterating the front path. The garden gate seemed to have been ripped out by somebody—you could see holes, where the hinges must have been—and the entire right-hand side of the frontage was obscured by one hugely overgrown bay-tree, as high as the gutters and almost as black. Up over the ridge-tiles, you could see the tops of yet more trees, so obviously no-one had cut anything back or cared about the place for years.

I brought my eyes back down again, still looking for clues about that noise.

Up in the window of the top left-hand-corner, there was a pair of rotting curtains—and in between them, I was sure I could make out the shape of a bare light bulb, just visible through the dirt on the glass. But that still didn't look like proof of current habitation. I scanned a bit lower, and eventually, downstairs, on the bottom bit of that peculiar sunburst design in the front door, I spotted what looked like a piece of paper taped onto the glass from the inside. I considered going up the path, to see if this was some kind of a message—but those brambles were really reaching out for each other across the path, and I was worried they might grab me.

There was another tree, I noticed, right up by the front door. Some sort of a wild sapling, it was, sickly-looking and straggly. Almost six feet high—and I couldn't help wondering how on earth it had managed to fight its way up through all those brambles, and how long the garden must have been left untended for it to have grown that tall. There was a butterfly, hanging around its branches; a Red Admiral, with winter-tattered wings.

Todd was six feet tall. Even when he took his shoes off.

I suppose what was troubling me most, as I stood there and stared at the front of this old house, was that I couldn't for the life of me work out why I'd never noticed it before. After all, my feet had taken me this way to the station almost every weekday for the last seven years, and houses don't become derelict overnight, do they? They don't just *arrive*. And what about the noise? Or rather; the voice.

I was absolutely sure you see that what had stopped my feet in their tracks that morning *was* a voice, and that it had been calling out to me from somewhere inside this filthy old house.

But equally obviously, now that I inspected it, it looked as though the house had been empty for—what? Weeks? Months? Years?

I just couldn't work it out at all.

Specifically, I couldn't think of anyone who'd assume they had the right to shout at me like that, or to use my actual name— because that was very definitely what the house had done. I mean; who on earth? Everyone knows that you have to be careful with your choice of words around the recently bereaved. Careful not to be over-familiar, especially.

I looked back up to that upstairs window with the curtains again, then brought my eyes back down to the splitting black paint of the front door—across the rusted letter-box—and right down to that taped-on message. Nothing. No signs of current life at all. I thought about it, and decided that I must just always have been too busy to notice the place. On the way to work, I would have been thinking ahead to my day; on the way home, I would have been thinking about him.

Remembering that made me look down at my watch, and looking down at my watch made my feet move fast, because it was now one minute to seven—and when I got there—to the station—I tell you, I was glad I'd remembered my season-ticket, because none of the automatic ticket-machines were working—can you believe it—and if I'd had to stoop down and shout things through that infuriating little microphone-thing that they now have fitted to the bottom of the ticket-office window, well I think things would have got even more tangled than they were already.

By the time we reached Clapham Junction, the train was full, and I had to spend the last ten minutes with the crotch of some-body's trousers practically inches from my face. I tried shutting my eyes, but that made both the voice and that poor damaged butterfly come back to me at the same time, and I started to feel properly sick again. I was even starting to plan how I might best barge my way to a toilet, but then, as we finally pulled past what's left of Battersea Power Station, things subsided, and so I just sat tight.

At Victoria, I let everybody else get off first (including the man whose trousers had been in my face). I knew that everybody in the office was going to look up and stare at me the minute I walked in, and I felt the need to gather myself for a moment before I committed to getting on the Victoria Line.

So yes, that was how I found the empty house on Christchurch Road.

§

Our office is on Candover Street, so ten minutes from Oxford Circus tube-station, pretty much. Just round the corner from the site of the old Middlesex Hospital, if that helps? We're a small company, specialising in air-freight—hence Sea Wings being the name—and it's my job to handle foreign-language correspondence. Which means invoice queries, mostly. We work largely with the Cote d'Ivoire, but also with Senegal, the Islamic Republic of Mauritania and sometimes with Algeria.

People *were* surprised when they saw me. My colleague Sheila in particular looked actually shocked. As it turned out, that was mostly because of the blood. I'd cut my neck while shaving myself in that broken mirror, you see, and the cut had somehow managed to open itself up again on the train. Anyway, I went and cleaned myself up a bit—Sheila calmed down—and then

I'm glad to say that neither she nor anybody else tried to say anything much to me at all. A temporary girl called Elaine did lean forward just after coffee-time and ask me how I was doing—which meant I suppose that people had been talking about me—but I simply told her as politely as I could that I thought I was doing just fine, and that I had an urgent query from Abidjan to deal with, so would she please excuse me.

Once my fingers had got over the oddity of being back at a keyboard, I didn't have to invent too much to fill up that first day. I spoke to Mr Harding, who's our boss, and he did mention compassionate leave still being available, but we soon got that out of the way.

Looking back, the only really tricky part of the day was sitting on the train home and realising as I was crossing the Thames again that the silence would probably be just then lifting its snout to the kitchen clock and calculating how many minutes it had left to wait for me. Plus—of course—I now had this house to walk past. I thought about just avoiding Christchurch Road altogether, but as the train got closer to home I decided it would be better to confront the issue head on.

If anything, the overgrown bay-tree seemed even bigger. I was very aware of its bulk, and that rank smell that the leaves acquire as they get older—but with a bit of an effort I got myself safely past, and without even really flinching. There was no repeat of that odd noise or voice trying to get at me from somewhere inside.

Or whatever it was, that had actually happened earlier.

In fact, there were pretty much no noise-related incidents at all that evening, and there was no repetition of anything really out of the ordinary on either of the remaining days of that first week. The closest I ever got to providing myself with an explanation of what had really happened with the house—and this was after a couple of scotches, on the Friday night—was when I decided that it had probably shouted at me simply because it recognised a fellow traveller. I mean, we'd both been abandoned.

Just for your information, I was downing at least two tumblers of Johnny Walker a night at this point, and not really eating anything of significance at all.

§

Now I'm going to jump to the very end of May.

Up in the flat, the silence was now starting to behave itself quite a lot better. Also, I think I was starting to take marginally better care of myself. On a couple of mornings, for instance, I even made myself some toast. Then, one lunchtime, Sheila—who is the only person who has worked for Sea Wings longer than I have, and certainly the only person there who is anything approaching a friend—Sheila asked me if it would be alright if she took me out for a sandwich. Wanting to dodge the inevitable questions that would follow if I told her that I still wasn't really eating at lunchtime, I said of course she could. And so at one o'clock we walked across to the steps of All Soul's together, via her usual sandwich place on Wells St.

I never have been the sort of person who assumes other people's lives are much like mine; however, over the years, I have developed considerable skills in going along with that fiction as and when required. And so, after we'd found a suitable spot on the steps, and sat down in the sun, and unwrapped our respective lunches, it really wasn't too hard for me to nod appropriately as Sheila listed all the things she said she was sure I must be going through. She talked about time being a natural healer, and how it changes everything—or as she rather unfortunately capitalised it, how Time Changes Everything, as in the one song on the radio that always made Todd absolutely *roar* with loathing—and then, when she saw that my ham and cheese sandwich was still unbitten-into, she talked about how my appetite was bound to return eventually. Also, she said, she'd recently been reading online that having photographs of the deceased dotted around your living space can be a genuine help. Because they give you someone to talk to, she said, and had I considered that as a possible way forwards? The trick works—Sheila added—for really all sorts of relationships.

When she'd finished, I waited a moment, and then said I'd consider her suggestions. At which point, Sheila grabbed my hands—and I mean she literally grabbed them, knocking half the coffee I'd been sipping down the church steps; then, she started talking very fast, telling me all about what a wonderful man Todd had been, and how good it was that we'd been together all those years, and how especially marvellous it was that we'd managed to find each other back in what she called *the bad old days*.

Sheila said all of these things to me as if she'd really known the man, whereas in fact I knew she'd only met Todd half a dozen times at most, and then only at office parties. Not knowing what else to do, I flung her hands away, put down my paper cup, and leaned forward and hugged her very hard. She burst into tears, but at least she stopped talking.

I know that Sheila means well—I really do—but what she couldn't possibly know that lunchtime was that when your husband dies, there's no safety anywhere. Not on the street; not in the sun; not anywhere.

That night, I got very drunk indeed. When I finally made it upstairs, I forgot to turn the lights off, and ended up lying there for what seemed like almost another day. Also, I had to listen to the silence, trying first of all to stifle its laughter at my predicament, and then giving up and letting rip at me completely.

I still made the seven-o-nine train the next morning, however.

§

Sheila was right about one thing; my appetite did return.

The first time I realised this was beginning to be the case would have been the next Friday. As I walked home from the station that evening (barely even looking at the empty house, this time) I found myself wanting to get back to the flat in order to eat something, whereas normally at that point in my homewards journey I would only have been looking forward to the first of my two Johnny Walkers. So once I got three corners away from the seafront, I detoured via Portland Street and went into the corner shop there and bought myself a packet of halloumi. Also, a small jar of mayonnaise, an iceberg lettuce and two more-or-less ripe tomatoes. When I got home, I not only made myself two large home-made sandwiches, I even ate them off a plate.

The next morning, I got myself dressed almost immediately. I found the car-keys, and drove out to our largest edge-of-town supermarket, the one Todd and I always used for our Saturday morning food-shopping. Now, of course, I wonder what on earth I can have been imagining. I mean; did I think the house wouldn't have counted the number of times that I'd now walked past it and not even bothered to look up at its dirty windows and check for signs of life? Did I really think it wouldn't try and get its own back?

§

Do you ever have that dream where everything's been moved, but nobody has told you why? Well, that's *exactly* what it was like.

Nothing on the shelves was where I remembered it as having been, for starters. And then, when I did manage to finally locate whatever product it was that I'd been looking for, there seemed to be far too much choice of everything. I managed to fill about half of my trolley, doing the best I could, but eventually I found myself pushing it down an aisle lined with absolutely nothing but different brands of fruit juice. And I'm afraid that made my feet do their involuntary stopping act again.

It also made me bite down on my lip rather badly, and I had to get out my handkerchief to check that there wasn't any actual blood.

When Todd was in the hospice, you see—and this would have been in mid-February, after he went in on the 8th—you never knew if he was going to ask for orange juice or cranberry, in the morning. Which meant—obviously—that I had to make sure the nurses always had both options standing by in his personal fridge. And now, here I was, surrounded by all of these cartons, and I was getting absolutely no help from him at all in locating the right ones. D'you see? And I was doing the best I could, trying to resolve all of the different kinds of packaging into some sort of a system, or to at least get them colour-coded, when suddenly this young manager-person comes right up behind me and asks me out loud if he can help. And the trouble is, he uses that very particular voice they all have—you know, the one which assumes that just because you have grey hair and a bit of a stomach then you must be either demented or deaf. Or both. And something about the way that he did that to me made me instantly and ab-solutely need to get out of there—I mean it really made me quite unreasonably ticked off. He asked me again, but I didn't reply, I just started lunging at things and filling my trolley up pretty much regardless. Which caused a spot of shouting. And that reminded me of the voice from inside the house, you see—which I know wasn't that young man's fault, but still—and so much so, in fact, that by the time I was queuing for the checkout I'd even convinced myself that he'd also used my actual name. All of which palaver meant that by the time I'd got home, and hauled all the carrier-bags up the stairs, I discovered that I'd bought far too much of everything.

And I mean not just fruit juice.

Eggs, for instance; first, I found a pack of a dozen large, which I'd managed to crack, and then, in another bag completely, I discovered that I'd also bought a whole extra half-dozen medium. I'd bought *two* of those six-packs of chopped tomatoes, which is more than the two of us could have got through in a month, even when Todd was still eating properly, and also two whole litres of milk, both full-fat, which neither of us had ever used anyway. Three tins of beans; two bunches of bananas; two of those infuriatingly plastic-boxed sets of pears. And so on. As a result of which, Todd's lovely black marble-effect worktop in the kitchen was soon completely covered in bags and packaging—and then, when I turned round, I discovered that there were still three more overflowing carrier-bags right there at my feet. Which was ridiculous.

Obviously.

I held on to the edge of the marble for a moment, and tried to breathe.

At this point, the silence—which hadn't been plaguing me so much recently, as I said, but which had obviously just been growing its claws somewhere out of sight, and now fancied a proper tussle—well at this point, the silence decided it was time to really make its presence felt. I could hear it scratching and giggling away somewhere behind me—and so before I started putting away all of my unnecessary tins of tomatoes in the top kitchen cupboard, I turned on the radio, thinking that some music might at least keep it occupied. But what came on, of course, was an orchestra—and one that had strings absolutely bloody everywhere. To get over this problem, I told the silence—out loud, and from up on my chair—that I was surprised it hadn't heard that when somebody was called away suddenly, it was perfectly normal for the person who'd been left behind to require some time. In fact—I announced, over the scrabbling strings—it was absolutely usual for the left-behind person to require as much time to get used to living on their own again as it had once taken them to get used to living with somebody else in the first place—which wasn't one of my lines at all, but was something that Sheila had spouted at me in the course of our lunchtime on Langham Place. And I knew it was bollocks—or at least, that it certainly didn't apply to Todd and me, because he and I were basically sorted after our very first night together—but anyway, there I was, cupboard doors all open, and feeling pretty bloody defenceless as it happened, and so I scrambled down off the chair and turned up the orchestra, hoping, I suppose, that maybe the silence wouldn't be able to get a word in edgeways if the violins got loud enough. It helped, and after a bit I was able to turn the music down again and carry on with my unpacking.

I think now that turning the radio down like that must have lulled me into some sort of a false sense of security, because even as I was opening the cutlery drawer, I still didn't see what was coming next. Really, I didn't see it coming at all—and now of course I can see that I absolutely should have.

To understand this next bit, you need to know that Todd always kept his lemons for cooking in a bowl out on the worktop, rather than in the fridge. It was a big, plain white china bowl, one that I'd given him back in our early days, and which he loved to use for this particular job because it contrasted so handsomely with the shiny soft black of his marble. Also, yellow always was his favourite colour, and the white of this particular china showed off the yellow of lemons to perfection—and so naturally, this was the bowl I'd got ready to put them in this morning. And then, when I couldn't get the little plastic mesh bag that the lemons were in to tear open with my teeth, I'd equally naturally thought of looking for our kitchen scissors. So I put the bag of lemons down, I opened the cutlery drawer—and that's when all hell broke loose. Maybe it was the brightness of those particular lemons, or the whiteness of Todd's bowl, or the sunlight of that morning; I still don't especially know. But what I do know for certain is that the sight of my hand hovering over the open cutlery drawer while I looked for our scissors made me quite literally see Todd's hand doing the same thing. And I mean actually his fingers, with both of his rings, and also exactly his fingernails. And then, as if that wasn't bad enough, all of the metal things down in the drawer there started singing. The knives, especially. I stared, and shouted, but everything went black-red all of a sudden, and I had to grab on to the edge of the worktop again in order to stop myself from going right over. The bowl got knocked off onto the floor somehow, and I heard it smash, and then—I suppose because I'd just broken his favourite bowl, or something—Todd started shouting at me. And I mean he wasn't coming at me from a distance this time, from a dirty window across the road or from behind me on a supermarket aisle, oh no, he was really right there next to me in my own kitchen, and shouting at the very top of his voice. I tried shouting back at him, of course, telling him how hard I was trying, and how all the extra food I'd bought was only because I wanted him to get strong again for his next round of chemotherapy, but it was no use. Then the other noises started, the ones I thought I'd got over making by now, and at that point I had to slide down onto the floor amongst all the broken china and bite down on one of the spare carrier-bags, just to get my mouth back under control.

Later, when things had settled down a bit, I worked out where all of that must have come from.

One Saturday morning, we were unpacking our shopping (this would have been last December, when Todd was still well enough for us to do our regular weekend shopping trips together) and while we were sorting everything out and putting things away, there'd been a discussion programme on the kitchen radio. It was just on in the background, like always, and we were happily getting things out of the bags and stowing them away together—and he was the one up on the chair that morning, I remember, not me—when the panel on the radio started talking about Change. With a capital letter. And two of the speakers started to disagree quite seriously about how it actually happens, Change, and eventually things all got quite shouty. One of the panellists said that everybody knows that things in this country only ever alter very slowly, and so I said that I thought she had a point—and as soon as I said that, Todd joined in and started shouting as well. Not at her, would you mind, but at me, right over the noise of the radio. And he wasn't actually angry, of course, because Todd was never *really* angry with me, not even when things got truly terrible towards the end of his treatment—but, Honestly darling, he shouted down from his chair, something tells me you've been working in that bloody office of yours too long. And he was busy reaching up to the top cupboard while this was happening, you see, using exactly the same chair that I'd just been using to stow away all those wretched tomatoes. I reckon it's about time we took you on a demonstration again, he yelled down at me—because he used to do that to me sometimes, you see, in our early years, take me on demos and marches with his colleagues—and the thing was, when he shouted at me in the kitchen last year, Todd's voice still had plenty of all his usual fun and laughter mixed into it, but now, this year, I mean on that Saturday, all of those things had gone from his voice entirely, and the only thing he seemed to have left for me was the sound of somebody genuinely wanting to cause pain. Like he wasn't angry about his broken china bowl at all, but had just been waiting for the right excuse to hurt me.

The noise subsided. I pulled the plastic bag out of my mouth, took some deep breaths—but even then, I still found that I had to stay down on my hands and knees in order to get myself safely into the living room. When I finally made it, I couldn't get my bottle of Johnny Walker open, and somehow the neck on the bottle turned into the neck of that assistant manager, and I shook him till he spilt all over the carpet.

The next thing I remember is that carpet being under my face still, and the sunset creeping in under my living-room curtains. And that made me remember those other ones, the ones in the filthy upstairs window, with that naked light-bulb dangling down between them.

D'you see?

§

Next Monday lunchtime, Sheila announced she was retiring. This was a surprise, because everyone at Sea Wings thought of Sheila as being rather a fixture—but everyone also agreed that this shift in her life really ought to be marked by some kind of a celebration. And so that Friday evening, we all met up in the Battersea Arms, which is our local. The Arms is a typical just-off-Oxford-Street kind of a pub—mirrors everywhere, lots of Victorian cut glass—and on a Friday night especially there's always quite a bit of shouting as well. Lots of men sweating into their collars and ties; lots of women, starting to shriek.

That Friday was no exception; the place was absolutely heaving, and after three large scotches I found myself staying much longer than I really should have. I got chatting to a young guy who'd recently joined the company, and think I may have even laughed out loud with him at one point and let myself hang an arm around his shoulder. When it got to last orders, Sheila kissed me on both cheeks, and said she was really glad to see me turning the corner at last. Then she hugged me, and I could feel each of her fingers digging into my arms through the sleeves of my jacket—and I know Sheila means well, as I've said before, but afterwards I felt I really had to go down to the gents and wipe the lipstick off my face. Everything down there was wet, and filthy, and I suppose I must have missed my footing and slipped.

Anyway, somebody else came in shortly afterwards, and they helped me to get back upstairs. Because it was hot, and Friday, I'd tried to pull my tie down to half-mast; looking in one of the mirrors, I saw that I'd actually torn a couple of buttons off my shirt. Nobody said anything, and I remembering laughing into my glass and wondering if they were all still sorry for me.

At Victoria, I had to sit on a bench for what felt like ages, and so by the time I was finally walking back down Christchurch Road god knows what o'clock it was.

The bay tree was very big, and very black, and as I came down the road I could smell it even more strongly than ever.

Foxes, I thought to myself. Maybe even jackals. Hyaenas.

My feet stopped; I swayed, ever so slightly—and then I tried to pull up my tie again. I could feel the house staring right back at me, you see, disapproving of me from behind all of its dirty glass. And then, just for a moment—and I mean literally just for one second—I was absolutely sure that I'd seen something moving up there behind that filthy window. The one at top left, I mean, with those rotting curtains and the light-bulb. Now I knew that the idea of there being somebody up there was crazy, Friday night or not, because there'd never been so much as a single sign of life from the place, not since that very first incident with the shouting voice—and so, after a quick second look and a glare back at the house in general, I spat out the smell of the bay-tree, spun myself around, and told myself not to be so bloody stupid. And then—no sooner had I done that—than my feet did another one of their involuntary dance-steps, and sent me staggering back up Christchurch Road towards the station again.

There's bound to be a way in round the back, somebody whispered in my ear. *You know what these old places are like*, the whisperer said. *They all have a way in round the back somewhere, especially after a couple of drinks.*

§

There was a hedge, with wet leaves—privet, I think it was—and those leaves stank as well. Then, the voice was right; you pushed your way in through a half-hidden gap, and then, next thing you knew, you found yourself standing at the top of some sort of a narrow, brick-paved alleyway, one that was offering to lead you down between the backs of the houses. It had high, leaning walls, this alleyway, and down at the bottom there, on the side, there was what seemed to be a garden gate. I say seemed, because things were in almost complete darkness by the time I'd got down that far down. I had to use my hands in order to find the right place to set my shoulder, and things slipped, and I swore, because the wood was so slimy—but eventually, there was a loud cracking noise, and I was in.

The darkness seemed almost solid, now.

However, there was still a path, and I could feel its bricks beneath my feet. I got slowly clear of the overhanging trees, and looked up. I could see ridge-tiles, silhouetted against a yellow glow, and I knew this had to be coming from the street-lamps over on the other side of the house. Straight up ahead of me, there was something that looked pale and cut up into squares. I stepped forward—slowly, because there were brambles here too—and discovered that the rectangle was a door, and those squares its panes of glass. I took my jacket off—the arms managed to get themselves all twisted together, like a pair of am-ateur-night wrestlers, which made me laugh under my breath—but after a bit of a struggle, I got the cloth safely wrapped round my fist and forearm.

Whoever would have thought that a person three years away from retirement would be so good at breaking and entering, eh?

The pane I'd chosen went in easily—the noise it made was more like a snap, than a smash—and so I unwrapped my hand and started reaching down inside. I was dreading a kiss to the inside of my wrist from some jealous piece of broken glass, but actually my fingers found the first of the locks just fine. They twisted it, and at the same time my other hand was turning the outside handle, trying to get the two things to work together.

Well this is all a bit like fucking, I thought to myself, and laughed again. First you press; then you shift a bit; then you press harder...

I groped downwards, and eventually my fingers found a second lock. This one had a key. I swore, because the key seemed stuck, but I twisted the metal as best I could—and suddenly something down inside there shifted. *Open sesame*, said the voice in my ear. My fingers crawled back up again, and I twisted the top lock too. The kiss never came, and the door swung open.

At first, there were just stray gleams of light coming off what looked like the handles of some old-fashioned cupboard units, with maybe a stainless-steel draining-board at the back. Then, slowly, my eyes began to make out a table, bare-topped, and what looked like a step up towards another door. I reckoned that was where I needed to get to, so I walked carefully round the table towards it.

Up the step—through this next door (it stuck, at first, and creaked)—and then the light out there in the hallway was all in the same sort of dull yellow which I'd seen coming up over the roof. I stood still for a bit, and watched some shapes lying on the carpet up by the front door turn themselves into a pile of old mail. I stepped over a piece of trailing flex, and realised that a darker shape, outlined on the lowest bit of the door's sunburst, must be the taped-on message that I'd seen from out on Christchurch Road. When I got to it, the paper was brittle, and broke into fragments in my hand; there'd clearly once been an address and telephone number scrawled across the top, but the writing was much too faded now to read. The mail seemed to be just old pieces of advertising—brochures from take-outs, with pictures of food that must have gone cold years ago. When I turned around, the yellow light from the street-lamps was only getting to about halfway up the stairs; above that, I could see nothing.

The palm of my hand went very smoothly and slowly up the bannister, and the white paint felt as dry and hot as somebody else's skin.

I knew that the bedroom with the lightbulb had to be just around to my left, but I also knew that I had to take things slowly; once I'd let go of the banister, I was going to be completely in the dark. I groped—there was a curious smell at this point, like clothes that hadn't been changed for far too long—and then, once they'd spider-crawled their way into and out of the corner, my fingers found what they were looking for. First of all, there was a door-frame; then, after another seven or eight inches, there was a door-handle. But there didn't seem to be a light-switch, not out here, and so at the same time as I was turning the handle and pushing the door open I was also automatically reaching round inside the room in order to try and find one there. I didn't think, when I did this; it was a move my body made for me. If I'd thought about it, I suppose I would have assumed that the power in the house must have been long-since disconnected, and not bothered. As it was, when my fingers did finally find a light-switch, and flick it down, it then took my brain at least a couple of seconds to work out what had just happened. The power was on. The glare from the lightbulb punched at my eyes; my fingers moved as quickly as they could to restore the room to darkness, but they were too slow, because I'd already seen what was in there.

It was a man—and barely ten feet away from me. As if I'd surprised him in the middle of some appalling meal, he was lifting his face towards me in confusion; he did it like an animal would, if disturbed in the middle of gutting something. He looked to be about my height and age; he had my own greying hair, and a pair of red, out-of-focus eyes. He was wearing a dishevelled jacket, and his shirt-collar had been yanked open to reveal a stringy and muscular neck. The skin of his face was ashen, and his mouth was hanging open to show a set of wet and yellowing canines. He staggered towards me—the mouth started to gape wide—and I started to scream.

Of course, it was me; me, reflected in a dust-blurred bedroom window. But Christ, those were a bad few seconds in my life. And what made them worse—what made me lean up against that filthy bedroom wall in the dark and shake like a lunatic while I stuffed my fingers in my mouth to try and stop myself from screaming—what made them worse, was knowing that if some stranger had been walking past at that moment, out on Christchurch Road, and had looked up, then they could have seen me. And when they saw me, they would have thought that I lived there. They would have thought that the sweating and open-mouthed creature they could see up there—this screaming and incontinent *thing*—was who I had now actually become.

§

The next morning, there was quite a bit of evidence. There were several deep scratches across my calves, and a nasty graze on the inside of my right palm, all of which I suppose I must have acquired when the brambles in the house's back garden had tried to bring me down as I fled. However, by the time that I'd finished my second Saturday coffee, I'd somehow managed to persuade myself that the whole thing had been just another one of my bad patches. I told myself that I really needed to cut down on my drinking, and then I turned on the news. Somebody on the radio was explaining that almost everything in this country was about to get much better, very soon.

And then, the next Monday evening, I retraced my steps.

That's right; like a dog, to his vomit.

§

It was early evening, and the back garden was already mostly in shadow. However, once I got inside again there was a kind of underwater light in that old-fashioned back kitchen which somehow made entering the house feel easier. In the hall, I picked up the faded flyers again—and this time I found a couple of old envelopes as well. They were addressed *To the legal owner*—and I was glad, because if there had been an actual name written on any of them then I think the sight of that might have sent me stumbling away again at once. The house felt weirdly vulnerable, in this half-light, and being reminded that it had once been somebody's home might have made me lose my nerve.

I braced myself, at the top of the stairs—I really couldn't help it—but then I just took a deep breath and stepped left. There was a faint smell of kicked-up dust, in the bedroom, and the door was still wide open, but apart from that you would never have known it had been disturbed. Or even that it had been much lived-in in the first place, as it happens, because there was no bed in there; no pictures, or a bedside table. Nothing but the lightbulb itself, and that pair of faded, rotting curtains. I thought of trying the light-switch again, to see if the power really was still on, but as soon as I tried to move my fingers up the wall towards it they let me know that they didn't really want to do that. I closed the door quietly.

The next bedroom along—the one in the rear left-hand corner of the house—was rather gloomy. The window had been pasted over with sheets of old newspaper for some reason, and the smell in here was of damp. There was a water-stain, spreading across the ceiling, and the ceiling itself looked as though it was about to lean down and greet me. I left the room to itself, and kept going. I just needed to check that the upstairs of the house was as empty as it looked, I told myself, and then I could go quietly back home to my own flat and forget this whole business.

The next door opened onto a bathroom. The glass in here had been obscured with whitewash, not paper, and the paint was now starting to flake away. You could see smudges of sunlight, trying to prise their way through, and I worked out that they must have been making their way through the tops of the trees out in the back garden. I wondered who'd painted over their bathroom window like that, and why. I wondered when anyone had last been naked in here. The water in the toilet-bowl was rusty, and foul.

I don't know what I was expecting to find behind the third and final door—more dust, I suppose, and probably more newspaper or paint over the window. I can remember thinking again to myself that this was the very last room in the house that I needed to check, and that as soon as I'd peeked in here it would finally be time to take myself away. However, when I pressed open the door, the room wasn't empty at all.

There was light—everywhere. Golden, thick-muscled light. The ceiling and the wall across from the window looked almost as if they'd been gilded, and the air, which was full of slowly dancing dust, looked molten. As I watched it shift, and coalesce, I began to work out that the room was being stencilled with a thousand, slowly-shifting circles—a thousand coins, or maybe sequins— and that this was the effect of a sort of multiple pin-hole camera that was being created by the sunset and the leaves of the trees outside. I stood in the doorway for a bit, watching these beautiful shapes endlessly rearrange themselves, and then I walked right into the middle of the space and let the light print itself all over me as well. It spangled my hands, and my wrists, and my clothes. After a while, I stepped even further forward, and cleared a patch of dirt from the window with the tips of two fingers.

I discovered that from up here, the trees in the back garden looked even bigger and wilder than they had from down below. Their leaves were congested, and dark—and because they were keeping everything else hidden—all of the neighbouring houses, and all of their windows and doors—you suddenly realised just how extraordinarily private this room was. How it wasn't silent, or rather not in the stifling way that my flat was silent, but actually *quiet*; how it was, in a way, just breathing very gently to itself. I could have taken all of my clothes off, I suddenly felt, and not a person in the world would have been able to see me do it. No one would have reprimanded me; no one would have started shouting that I shouldn't be so stupid or undignified. No one would have told me to be more appropriate, or careful.

As well as having its own and very special light, this final room was also different in that it hadn't been entirely emptied of its furniture. Whoever had last moved out had left behind them a big old double mattress, propped up against the wall opposite the window. You could see from the four black pressure-marks down on the carpet where the bedstead itself would once have stood, and even though this mattress was now all stained, and even torn in one or two places, you could still imagine how well-arranged the room must once have been. They would have spent hours up here, I thought, the people who had lived here. Hours, just lying on their bed—in this light—and there would have been no noise at all.

I wonder why they didn't take the mattress with them, I thought. I mean; who leaves their bed behind?

I stayed up there in the light for pretty much a whole hour, that first time. Just sitting on the floor, with my back against the mattress there, and watching the circles moving into new configurations and the walls getting slowly darker. When I left, my trousers were snagged by a new spray of bramble, one which was just starting to reach across the kitchen doorway. I lifted it carefully back into place behind me, and then relocked the door. It's amazing how fast they can grow, those brambles, and just how green and soft to the touch the newly-developed spines are.

§

The first real change I made was to move that mattress. It wasn't easy, because the blasted thing was so heavy, but at least I didn't have to get it up or down any stairs. Once I'd got it manoeuvred down onto the floor, I then just pulled and pushed it across the carpet until I'd got it resting with its head against the wall and its four corners aligned with those four black marks on the carpet. It seemed right, somehow, to put it back pretty much where it would have been originally. I brought two pillows and pillowcases from home, to make things a little more comfortable, and also two bottles of water from the Portland Street corner-shop. The next evening, I rescued a discarded Evening Standard from the floor of my homeward train, and spread it out next to the mattress as a sort of improvised bedside table for the bottles.

I didn't mind at all that the mattress itself was still bare; in fact, I found its old-fashioned smell of mattress-ticking oddly reassuring. I usually started my visits by lying on my back for a bit, and then, as the light shifted, I would go over onto my side, with my knees up and one arm crooked under my head on the pillow. I always lay on the left-hand side of the bed—my side—and sometimes, but not often, I used to push my hand down between my legs and then clamp them together for a bit as well. But never anything more.

I used to stay like that for ages, really, hardly moving at all, and just watching the sunlight. Once, I did start saying Todd's name out loud, and that upset me quite badly; but afterwards, I told myself it was fine, and reminded myself that there was no-one there in the house to hear or judge me. That definitely helped.

In July, I took my annual leave. The evenings got lovelier—and lighter, which meant that I now had to check for possible passers-by before I squeezed myself in through that gap in the privet hedge. With it being proper summer at last, I sometimes found after a visit that my handkerchief wouldn't suffice to get all the dust off my face and hands before I walked home to the sea-front. Because of that, I started keeping a damp towel at the house, rolled up in a supermarket carrier-bag. Eventually, I even got into the habit of taking in some bits of food along from the Portland Street corner-shop—only small things, pasties and such-like, and sometimes apples—but at least that way I never had to leave early on account of getting hungry.

The bramble at the back door grew thick and strong. One night, I took a knife and some putty, and quietly replaced the pane of glass that I'd broken in the back door. It seemed only polite.

My drinking was pretty much back under control now, I'm glad to say, and I was starting to sleep more or less normally. However, I still hadn't risked going back to the supermarket. There are plenty of smaller places to buy your groceries in, down here, so long as you don't mind walking around the town a bit, and I definitely didn't want to risk things going all haywire again.

And now we come to three days ago.

§

I'd been feeling for quite some time that it was remiss of me still not to have done anything at all with Todd's clothes, and now that my evenings spent at the house had calmed me down a bit, I thought that perhaps I was ready to start making that omission good. Besides, I was off work, I had the time—the charity shops down here always have signs saying they're grateful for good quality items—and everything did seem to have levelled out a bit. Even the silence was behaving itself.

I thought about jumping in at the deep end and starting with his suits—or even perhaps with his old leather jacket, the one that he'd insisted on never throwing away—but then, when it came down to it, I simply couldn't bring myself to open his side of the wardrobe. Instead of beating myself up about that, I decided to make a start by tackling the cupboard under the stairs. Clearing the cupboard under the stairs was one of quite a lot of things that we'd always said we'd get round to doing together, but then never actually had.

Once I'd started, I soon discovered the amount of stuff that we'd hidden away under there was ridiculous. I dug out an electric sewing machine (something that I couldn't remember either of us ever having used here in the flat); a whole second tool-box, full of nothing but nails and screws and two broken hammers; a box of old security locks; a big old printed-cotton Indian bedspread (something which I think Todd must have used to cover a wall in one of his very early places, before I'd even met him); a dozen rusted-up tins of gloss paint (two of them bright yellow) and four boxes of books in French. Presumably, I'd brought them with us when we'd moved in, but then had never even unpacked them.

I sorted and dragged stuff until I was filthy—it's a big cupboard, and deep—and then I put as much as I thought I'd have the energy to carry down to the car in the morning into four big black plastic bin-liners. Then I told myself that if I was going to be driving to a charity shop, then I might as well try calling in at the supermarket on the way home. I even stayed up and ironed a shirt—because that was what Todd and I always did when we did our Saturday shop together, put on clean shirts. We always made sure we looked smart together, us two.

It was nearly midnight by the time I'd done all of that, and I was tired. I crawled upstairs, completely forgetting to have my usual glass of whisky, and that night I really did sleep like a dog.

This next thing I'm going to try and tell you about is something that I really can't think straight about. Not yet, anyway. So please let me say in advance that I'm sorry if any of it comes out wrong. I think it had to happen, but I still wish that somebody else had done it, not me.

§

When I first saw him, he was standing in the next check-out queue along from me, and just about level to where I was in mine. He looked to be about fifty, maybe fifty-two—and I must say I hate being the age when you automatically notice that other men are a whole decade younger than yourself, but there you are. And of course, I straight away noticed his hair-colour.

He was wearing the same sort of smart Saturday-morning clothes as I was; jeans, and a dark blue, short-sleeved polo-shirt. He definitely looked like he'd also made an effort.

He turned around—and at first, I was confused by his expression. Then, when I saw that he really meant it—because he kept right on looking at me, and even risked the half-smile that's traditional on these occasions—well then I got angry. I even went red in the face, I think, which is something I never usually do, and had to bend over and rearrange some items in my trolley in order to try and break things up a bit and slow them down. Then, when it was time for me to stand back up again, the man had moved. He was a place ahead of me now, and that meant that I could see his back, and more of how well it fitted inside his shirt. What had appeared to be just plain dark red hair at first was actually a deep kind of copper-colour, I realised, and also that it shaded to a mysterious kind of almost-white at the shaving line on the back of his neck. He had very white skin, even on his copper-dusted forearms. He was a couple of inches shorter than me, and quite a bit better built. When you looked more closely, you also realised that he was probably only just in his late forties.

So he definitely wasn't Todd.

I mean, he wasn't Todd's age, he wasn't Todd's colouring, he didn't stand with one hip flexed, like Todd always used to—and believe me, I was going to turn away. But just as I started to do that, the man reached round to find his wallet, and the second smile that he gave me as he did that was even franker than the first. This one included his eyes—and now that he was doing that, I had time to notice that they were an extraordinary and completely unexpected blue.

Everything was moving very slowly, now, but also very fast. It had been so long since this had happened to me, you see, and really I couldn't remember how things were meant to go. I couldn't remember what the rules were, if that makes sense. I couldn't even remember how or when you were supposed to breathe—and I'm not saying that Todd and I didn't have our moments with other people, because we did, but eyes meeting across a crowded supermarket, well it had to be years since *that* had happened last.

In another country.

As they say.

I did look away, for just a moment—and then I looked back. And the man and his eyes were both still smiling. I thought about leaving, about walking away and just abandoning everything right where it stood—about saying to the woman at the till, I'm sorry, but I think I might've forgotten something. Or anything, really, to break up what was starting to happen to me. However, before I could do any of those things, the woman at the till called me forward. And I didn't want to be rude, so I bent down and starting putting my things onto the conveyor belt. And then, when I looked back up again, the red hair had disappeared. I scanned the exit, straight away, but I couldn't find anything in its sheets of glass except shadows and reflections.

I paid for my shopping, and thanked the woman. She looked as if she might be about to ask me how I was feeling, and so I moved away quite quickly. And then, when I got outside—and honestly, of all the stupid things that could have happened to me next, this was probably the worst—when I got outside again, with my trolley, I simply couldn't remember where I'd put the car.

I stood still for a bit, wondering what on earth was happening to me this morning, and then, telling myself that the incident was probably all over by now, and that I'd probably pretty much imagined the whole thing anyway, I decided that if I just pushed my trolley back to the shelter and reclaimed my pound coin then perhaps that might jog my memory. However, once I got to the shelter, the tag on the end of the chain—you know, that small metal bit you have to stick in the socket, in order to get your pound back—well the tag turned out to be bent. I pressed, and tugged, but it still wouldn't get itself all the way in—and then the whole stupid thing got jammed. I tugged—swore—kicked the trolley—hurt my foot—and that was when his voice touched me like a finger. Right on the back of my neck.

'Hi.'

The voice was friendly, even soft—but my hand still flew up to protect my face. He was standing with his back to the sun, and the light behind him was much too bright to look at.

'Nice morning to be out doing the shopping,' he said.

I knew that I had to respond; I knew that the air around us was warm, and that the colours were clear, and that the cars parked around us were all in orderly rows—and that he was just a few feet away from me, with his hands held casually down by his sides. I knew that no one was watching us. There was no shouting going on at all.

'I was just wondering, if—'

'Yes?'

'What you were doing after your shopping. Whether you were busy, so to speak.'

There was a pause, and I squinted into the light again. My mouth opened, but nothing useful came out.

'I—'

And that was really all I could manage. There were clouds, and the pattern of their shadows was shifting calmly across the parked cars; his eyes were still smiling—but none of that was helping me at all.

'I—'

I wanted badly to apologise. I wanted to shake myself awake, and explain; I wanted to say to this handsome and kindly-looking stranger, Sorry, but can't you tell? My husband died in the last week of March, and this is still only the first week of August. Do you see? And honestly, I would never have put on a clean shirt if I'd thought anything like this was going to happen—I wanted to say to him—because you see for you this may feel like just trying to pick up a stranger in a supermarket car-park, but for me it feels like standing on the edge of a cliff so high that it makes my stomach turn over. It makes me feel like my body belongs to someone else. It makes me want to fold myself up, and just not be here.

He waited, and smiled, having no idea at all of what I was thinking. Well, how could he?

'Sorry,' I managed, finally. 'This isn't really a good time.'

'OK,' he said, reluctantly. And then—I think—I suppose I must have smiled too. And that made him say *he* was sorry. Maybe some other time, he said, since we obviously lived in the same small town, and used the same supermarket, and were bound to bump into each other again sooner or later? His eyes turned a darker shade of blue, and I knew that in just a moment he was going to step forward and put his hand on my arm. The cliff edge gave way, and I fell.

Please, I said out loud as I drove myself left and right and left towards the derelict house on Christchurch Road; please, don't watch us, my darling.

§

It's August, and hot, and although the trees outside this particular bedroom are tall and shadowy, someone has still felt the need to screen what is about to happen in here from view; in order to achieve that, they've stretched a thin cotton Indian-print bedspread right across the window. You can still see where the hammer and tacks that were used to accomplish this task have been left scattered across the carpet. The room seems very still, after that particular noise, and the sunshine filtering in through the warm rust-and-black colours of the bedspread is turning its air into one ruddy, red-gold solid.

In the middle of this warm cube of colour, two men are standing facing each other across a bare and rather dirty-looking mattress. This mattress lies directly on the floor, with its head against a wall, and the men are measuring the distance it creates between them with their eyes. As it happens, they are both half-undressed already. They seem to have reached some kind of an *impasse* in their choreography for just a moment, but then—quite unexpectedly—the younger and slightly shorter of the two makes a very definite move; he stoops, unlaces his shoes, and removes his socks; he then shucks off his trousers and underpants in one smooth and beautiful gesture. The older man attempts to follow suit, but when the moment comes for him to slip down his own underwear he feels obliged to turn around and present his back. Then he seems to pause for a moment, taking some apparently much-needed time to gather himself together before he turns back round to face his partner. When he does turn, his body is visibly thinner than the younger man's, and more worn; you can see every one of his sixty-two years, even though the light in this room seems determined to be kind. Both of the men are sweating already, because of the day's heat.

The staring between them continues for some time, but then—eventually—something moves again. It is a hand, this time—and now the shorter of the two men, the bloodily-haired one, steps forward onto the mattress and places this reaching hand of his first on the other man's arm, and then onto his left shoulder. When he feels this hand, the older man smiles, but still only with half of his mouth. He closes his eyes. The redhead, sensing that he must proceed very gently, moves his lips and face forwards in order to plant the softest of kisses on the other man's mouth. This kiss seems to be a question; eventually—and quietly—it receives a reply.

Once down on the mattress, their limbs seem to fit together quite well. Things move slowly, in this heat—but now, the questions being asked are no longer quite so tentative or gentle. Neither are their answers; the two men's eyes meet quite often now, closing only when they must, and when a head tips back or turns away it is not now with avoidance or refusal. When the time comes for more noise, the air of the room seems to absorb it all quite easily. For one of the two men the sounds that he is making turn unstoppably into tears, but fortunately his partner holds him tight when this happens, and lets the crisis pass without comment.

By the time they have both come, it is quite late in the afternoon, and the parti-coloured light that is still seeping through the bedspread has shifted several feet around their impromptu bedroom's walls. Both of their bodies are properly slicked with sweat now, and smeared with stripes of dust, and as they lie there side by side and stare up together at the ceiling—both of them feeling quite hollowed-out and silent now, as if they were lying together on some abandoned beach, listening perhaps to the waves of some distant and still-retreating tide—their bodies are contoured in several shades of a vivid and surprising colour. The light which is sculpting the face of the red-head discovers a line of pure carmine on the crest of both his cheekbones; his companion's skin takes the colour more gently. Again, a hand reaches out, and again it finds another. The red-head, who is on the right-hand side of the bed, turns, and it is he who begins the necessary conversation. 'Shall we do names, then?' he asks.

The older man keeps his eyes on the ceiling, and there is a considerable pause. When he finally does speak, you can still hear in his voice a record of all the weeping that he has just done, together with traces of all the other noises. 'Roger,' he says, hoarsely. 'I'm called Roger.'

'Hello Roger. My name's David.'

'Hello.'

There is a further silence here, quite a long one, and then the red-haired man tries again. 'I really needed that,' he says, quite cheerfully. 'How about you?' And then there is yet another silence—but the questioner persists. 'Are you alright, my friend?' he says.

§

Oh, I'd forgotten how it happens—the opening up, afterwards; the talking, while you both stare at the ceiling, and slowly try to come back to yourselves... And my god, how many times have I done that in my life, that I should have forgotten how it goes! We both had some water, and then David said he wished he had a cigarette, and laughed. And then I told him about Todd. Not everything—I didn't tell him Todd's name, for instance, or how long exactly he's been gone—but enough, because I wanted him to know at least that much about me. He touched me again at that point, on my face, which shocked me, and then he said he was sorry for my loss. I'd heard those words on the television of course, everyone has, but I think this was the first time I'd ever heard somebody say them in a voice that made me believe them.

None of it was easy.

We talked some more, and I found out that he's even younger than I'd thought—but not *so* young, because he has a son who's already a teenager. When he told me that, David got up off the mattress and went and fetched his wallet from his trousers—squatting unselfconsciously, so that his balls almost brushed the floor—and then came back with a photograph to show me. It's just a holiday snap, he said, from last year, when I saved up and took us both to Italy as a present for his making it through year ten. The photograph showed the boy leaping back against a breaking wave, all red and white and laughing, and looking straight into the camera. D'you see, David said, he's got his father's eyes and hair.

He's called Sean, the boy, and from the way David said that name you could tell straight away how much he loves him. I asked him what the story was, and he told me that he'd got married way too young, before either he or his wife had had the chance to find out who they really were. He said that it wasn't until after Sean had come along that they'd realised marriage wasn't the right thing for either of them. And then they'd both gone their own ways, he said, but he'd never for one moment considered leaving the boy behind. He looked at the picture again, and then told me it was funny how life turned out, because if anyone had ever said to him when he was younger that a fifteen-year-old boy would turn out to be the most beautiful and precious thing to him in the whole wide world, well then he wouldn't have had a blind idea what they were talking about that. Look at that skin, he said to me. There's no mistaking fifteen-year-old skin, is there, not even in a photograph?

Apparently his wife gets Sean every other weekend—hence this being his day to do the supermarket run—and when he used those words *every other weekend* you could hear in his voice how much it hurt him to be apart from the boy for even forty-eight hours. That was why he'd followed me out into the car park, he said, because he suddenly felt so lonely that he thought he might do himself an actual injury if he went home with his shopping all by himself. Then he asked me about the house—about Christchurch Road, I mean—about the mattress, and everything—and said did I own the place. When I said no, I'd just broken in, he laughed again, and said he didn't think he'd had sex in a derelict building since the turn of the century. I didn't ask him if he did this kind of thing often, and he didn't ask me that either.

When we were back downstairs in the kitchen, David pushed me up against the sink and kissed me really hard, pressing himself into me and really working to get my mouth fully open again. He was clumsy, and I was relieved in a way, because the clumsiness let me know that he wasn't the only one who was feeling way more than he could handle just at this minute. Then we walked back up the brick-paved alleyway together, and squeezed our way out through the gap in the privet-hedge. David turned right to find his car again, and I turned left to find mine.

Driving home, the strangest and perhaps loveliest thing of all wasn't remembering David himself, or how he'd looked after me while we were fucking, but the way he'd used his son's name. He'd said it almost straight away in our conversation—as if that was the point of the conversation, somehow—and once he'd started, he couldn't stop. It made me look forward to the time when I can start saying Todd's name out loud like that; to the time when I can start saying that name out loud to other people just as easily as David said his son's, and as gently.

It made me look forward to being able to say Todd's name as often as I think it, because now I know who I belong to, and who I always will.

So perhaps he hasn't left me after all.

§

There were no claws clicking their way across the hallway floor; there was no impatient whining from behind the door while I looked for my key. Once I was inside, I put my bags down, and listened very carefully, to check. Then, I went upstairs to the bathroom. The silence was still there, but it wasn't in charge any more.

It also felt considerably smaller.

I didn't want to challenge any of that, so I turned on the bathtaps rather carefully. As I got undressed, my first thought was that I'd somehow cut myself while I was thrashing around with David like that, because there appeared to be three great dreadful-looking weals or gashes right across my chest. But then I moved, and realised that these wounds were nothing to do with what had happened in the house, but rather just a trick of my broken bathroom mirror.

I could see some bruises, on my chest, and one set of marks from David's teeth lower down, but there was nothing to be too embarrassed about.

You're here now, I said to myself quietly. You're home.

While the bath was filling, I thought again about the final conversation that David and I had had before we parted, the one that had taken place on the pavement by the privet-hedge. He'd said to me that if we did decide that we wanted to see each other again, then he'd love to introduce me to his son. Sean's quite old enough to meet his father's friends, he said, and honestly these days things really are different. Teenagers these days, they're so much more clued up about life than you or I ever had the chance to be, he said, and if you were to come round, the three of us wouldn't need to pretend that anything is other than how it really is. Perhaps we could do dinner one evening up at my place, eh?

Turning off the taps filled the bathroom up with silence again, and I had to wait a moment for everything to settle down. Not tonight, I told myself, I won't call him tonight, but perhaps tomorrow.

I waited until the bath-water had turned itself into another mirror, and then I slid myself carefully down underneath. Under the water, *everything* came back—David's eyes, and his strength, and how I'd felt when I first realised that I was going to let myself come with a stranger. I remembered how helplessly I'd wept, afterwards, and then silently hoped that that particular thing would never happen to me again. I wondered if I would ever go back to the house; to all of those brambles, and to that peculiar smell of dust. Then my breath ran out, and I had to break the surface of the water.

After I'd dried myself, I went across the upstairs landing and into our bedroom. I opened the wardrobe—using both doors— and got myself properly dressed in some fresh, clean clothes.

Downstairs, something about the steady way the light was coming in off the sea made me stand for a bit and stare at it, and that made me think about David's son again, about him playing in the waves in that photograph. It made me wonder about what on earth it might be like to meet the boy in person. I tried to imagine what kinds of questions a fifteen-year-old might want to ask me about my life, and also what questions I might want to ask about his. About what this brave new world that we're all supposedly living in actually feels like, for somebody his age. I thought about his room—and about all the weird and unforgettable sense you have at that age of waiting for your life to properly begin. I thought about all the different rooms, and streets, and beds, and addresses. I looked at the sea, and the way the light out there was shifting yet again. Light never stays the same for long, does it?

§

That was yesterday.

A postscript;

On page 177, one of my characters says she thinks it's important to thank people who have helped you in your life, even if those people themselves may not be aware of exactly how they've done that for you. With that in mind, I think it would be wrong for me to end without thanking the people (all the living, and the dead...) whose real names and addresses I have borrowed for these stories, along with so much more besides. In Twickenham, thank you for everything, John; in Clerkenwell, thank you Jeffrey, Roberta, Derek, Ivan, Stuart, Keith and Lauren; also in Clerkenwell, thank you Miss Deacon (the loveliest of colleagues); in Hackney, a big thank you to Mr Kinsey, who's flat it really was, and also to Xardine, Vee, Zed, Dom, Peggy, Roman, Mr. O'Halloran and the lovely Mz Michelle; on Camden Road, thank you Ms Lennard, Mariette, Mrs Walker, Giardina and even (in a way) my grandfather's friend and colleague Roy Hobdell; in Ravenscourt Park, thank you Leo, and Harold, and Cyril, and Adjoa, and also thank you Lois. On Marine Parade, thank you to the Choudry family, thank you (and greetings) Mr Harding, hello across the years Elaine—and thank you, Sheila. A big thank you also to the landlord of No 8, and to the owner of the house on Christchurch Road, whatever your names were.

To James Gardiner, my thanks always and everywhere.

To Trevor, my father, who died just as I was finishing this—oh how I wish you could read it.

Neil Bartlett,
London/Worthing, 2021

Acknowledgements

My thanks to my indefatigable agent (and dear friend) Clare Conville, for all of her support; and of course to Justin and Nathan.

Neil

We would like to thank Alex Hopkins for proofreading, Daren Kay for copyrighting and our advisory board, particularly Rebecca Carter, Sam Missingham, Uli Lenart, Joe Mateo and Christopher Hamilton-Emery. Lastly and most importantly, our most sincere thanks to Neil Bartlett for getting on our magic carpet.

Justin David, *Publisher* & Nathan Evans, *Editor*
Inkandescent

Supporters

At Inkandescent, we believe books can save the world, particularly books of diversity. Stories make us feel less alone. They can educate. They can challenge us to reflect on different points of view. They can bring us great pleasure. Most importantly, stories help us to develop empathy. They make us better people—more socially, culturally and emotionally aware human beings, able to understand and feel compassion for voices different to our own.

It is widely known that mainstream publishing has consistently failed to raise up voices from a number of diverse groups; these are namely writers from LGBTQ+ and BAME backgrounds, those who are financially disadvantaged or who identify as working class. We started Inkandescent Publishing to provide a platform for underrepresented writers and artists.

We are small. Very small. But with the help of a growing readership, we have been able to publish ten books since 2016. Enough to fill a small bookshelf! The following list of names are people who supported the production of this book by pledging or pre-ordering a copy from our publishing partner, Unbound, long before the release date and to whom we are eternally grateful. For small indies like us, a bit of extra cash upfront means creative freedom. It means we can stop worrying about cashflow and balance sheets and instead focus upon bringing brilliant books to you. We have a lot more in the pipeline.

Whether the book you're holding in your hand was pre-ordered from Unbound or purchased more recently from a bookseller, we think you're inkredible! Because by buying one of our books you're helping to keep independent publishing alive.

THANK YOU!

Adjoa Andoh	Guy Foord-Kelcey	Patrizia Volta
Alan Wright	Huw Griffiths	Paul Crick
Andrew Fallaize	James Cronin	Paul Hicks
Andrew Nunn	James Hogan	Philip Ridley
Angela Clerkin	Jennifer Puchalla	Phillip Mackenzie
Ben Walters	John Atterbury	Piero Toto
Brian Mullin	John Lee Bird	Piers Torday
Brian Thorstenson	Jonathan Cohen	Ray Carne
Camilla Broadbent	Joshua Davis	Riccardo Durante
Carolyn Braby	Joyce Henderson	Robert Eardley
Charlie Beaumont	JV Bond	Robert Mcnicol
Christian Verdú Jouanneau	Kimberly Burke	Sameera Reyani
Craig Sills	Laura Longrigg	Sarah Morris
Dale Rapley	Laura Rees	Sarah Taylor
Damion Clark	Lawrence Schimel	Seán McGovern
David Leddy	Lin Hornby	Simon Casson
David Sheppeard	Liz Kettle	Simon Christie
Dominic Davies	Lois Keidan	Simon Maddrell
Don Shewey	Lynne Tillman	Simon Watney
E-J Scott	Marcus Romer	Stephen Pelton
Edward Clarke	Mark Southern	Steven Patterson
Elizabeth Pisani	Mark Vent	Tamzin Griffin
Emma Worrall	Martin J Gent	Tim Lethorn
Gary Davy	Matthew Bright	Tom Marshman
Gideon Lester	Matthew Foster	Tom Sargant
Gilbert Cohen-Solal	Michaela Varisto	Tony Timmons
Giles Havergal	Nando Messias	Trevor Norris
Graham Ward-Tipping	Nick Alexander	Tristan Williams
Greg Barnes	Nikki Milican	Turan Ali

Also from Inkandescent

THE PALE ONES
by Bartholomew Bennett

Few books ever become loved. Most linger on undead, their sallow pages labyrinths of old, brittle stories and screeds of forgotten knowledge... And other things, besides: Paper-pale forms that rustle softly through their leaves. Ink-dark shapes swarming in shadow beneath faded type. And an invitation...

Harris delights in collecting the unloved. He wonders if you'd care to donate. A small something for the odd, pale children no-one has seen. An old book, perchance? Neat is sweet; battered is better. Broken spine or torn binding, stained or scarred - ugly doesn't matter. Not a jot. And if you've left a little of yourself between the pages – a receipt or ticket, a mislaid letter, a scrawled note or number – that's just perfect. He might call on you again.

Hangover Square meets Naked Lunch through the lens of a classic M. R. James ghost story. To hell and back again (and again) through Whitby, Scarborough and the Yorkshire Moors. Enjoy your Mobius-trip.

'A real addition to the literature of the uncanny and an impressive debut for its uncompromising author.'
RAMSEY CAMPBELL

Also from Inkandescent

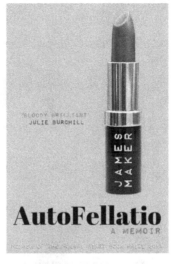

AutoFellatio
by James Maker

According to Wikipedia, only a few men can actually perform the act of auto-fellatio. We never discover whether James Maker—from rock bands Raymonde and RPLA—is one of them. But certainly, as a story-teller and raconteur, he is one in a million.

From Bermondsey enfant terrible to Valencian grande dame—a journey that variously stops off at Morrissey Confidant, Glam Rock Star, Dominatrix, Actor and Restoration Man—his long and winding tale is a compendium of memorable bons mots woven into a patchwork quilt of heart-warming anecdotes that make you feel like you've hit the wedding-reception jackpot by being unexpectedly seated next the groom's witty homosexual uncle.

More about the music industry than about coming out, this remix is a refreshing reminder that much of what we now think of as post-punk British rock and pop, owes much to the generation of musicians like James. The only criticism here is that – as in life – fellatio ultimately cums to an end.

'a glam-rock Naked Civil Servant in court shoes. But funnier.
And tougher' MARK SIMPSON

Also from Inkandescent

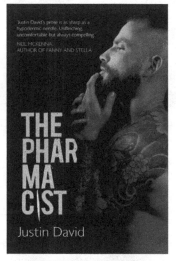

THE PHARMACIST
by Justin David

Twenty-four-year-old Billy is beautiful and sexy. Albert – The Pharmacist – is a compelling but damaged older man, and a veteran of London's late '90s club scene. After a chance meeting in the heart of the London's East End, Billy is seduced into the sphere of Albert. An unconventional friendship develops, fuelled by Albert's queer narratives and an endless supply of narcotics. Alive with the twilight times between day and night, consciousness and unconsciousness, the foundations of Billy's life begin to irrevocably shift and crack, as he fast-tracks toward manhood. This story of lust, love and loss is homoerotic bildungsroman at its finest.

'As lubricious as early Alan Hollinghurst, The Pharmacist is a welcome reissue from Inkandescent, and the perfect introduction to a singular voice in gay literature.'
THE TIMES LITERARY SUPPLEMENT

'At the heart of David's The Pharmacist is an oddly touching and bizarre love story, a modern day Harold and Maude set in the drugged-up world of pre-gentrification Shoreditch. The dialogue, especially, bristles with glorious life.'
JONATHAN KEMP

Also from Inkandescent

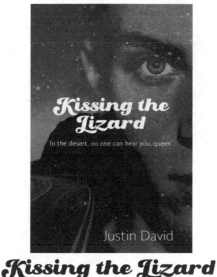

Kissing the Lizard

by Justin David

Justin David's newly-released novella is part creepy coming-of-age story, part black-comedy, set partly in buzzing 1990s London and partly in barren New Mexico wildlands.

When Jamie meets Matthew in Soho, he's drawn to his new-age charms. But when he follows his new friend across the planet to a remote earth-ship in Taos, bizarre incidents begin unfolding and Matthew's real nature reveals itself: he's a manipulative monster at the centre of a strange cult. Jamie finds himself at the centre a disturbing psychological nightmare as they seize the opportunity to recruit a new member. Pushed to his limits, lost in a shifting sagebrush landscape, can Jamie trust anyone to help him? And will he ever see home again?

This evocatively set desert gothic expertly walks the line between macabre humour and terrifying tension.

Also from Inkandescent

THREADS
by Nathan Evans & Justin David

If Alice landed in London not Wonderland this book might be the result. Threads is the first collection from Nathan Evans, each poem complemented by a bespoke photograph from Justin David and, like Tenniel's illustrations for Carroll, picture and word weft and warp to create an alchemic (rabbit) whole.

On one page, the image of an alien costume, hanging surreally beside a school uniform on a washing line, accompanies a poem about fleeing suburbia. On another, a poem about seeking asylum accompanies the image of another displaced alien on an urban train. Spun from heartfelt emotion and embroidered with humour, Threads will leave you aching with longing and laughter.

'In this bright and beautiful collaboration, poetry and photography join hands, creating sharp new ways to picture our lives and loves.'
NEIL BARTLETT

'Two boldly transgressive poetic voices'
MARISA CARNESKY

Also from Inkandescent

MAINSTREAM
edited by Justin David & Nathan Evans

'A wonderful collection of fascinating stories by unique voices'.
KATHY BURKE

This collection brings thirty authors in from the mar-gins to occupy centre-page. Queer storytellers. Working class wordsmiths. Chroniclers of colour. Writers whose life experiences give unique perspectives on universal challenges, whose voices must be heard. And read. Emerging writers are being placed alongside these established authors—

Bidisha, Elizabeth Baines, Gaylene Gould, Golnoosh Nour, Jonathan Kemp, Julia Bell, Keith Jarrett, Kerry Hudson, Kit de Waal, Juliet Jacques, Neil Bartlett, Neil McKenna, Padrika Tarrant, Paul McVeigh and Philip Ridley

'A riveting collection of stories, deftly articulated. Every voice entirely captivating: page to page, tale to tale. These are stories told with real heart from writers emerging from the margins in style.'
ASHLEY HICKSON-LOVENCE,
author of *The 392* and *Your Show*

by outsiders for outsiders

Inkandescent Publishing was created in 2016
by Justin David and Nathan Evans to shine a light on
diverse and distinctive voices.

Could you do one more Inkredible thing for us?
Sign up to our mailing list to stay informed
about future releases:

www.inkandescent.co.uk/sign-up

follow us on Facebook:

@InkandescentPublishing

on Twitter:

@InkandescentUK

and on Instagram:

@inkandescentuk